Little Jinx

Little Jinx

Abram Tertz

.

Translated by

Larry P. Joseph

and

Rachel May

With a Foreword by

Edward J. Brown

Northwestern University Press

Evanston, Illinois

This translation has been funded in part
by the National Endowment for the Arts.

Northwestern University Press
Evanston, Illinois 60201

Printed in the United States of America

First printing, 1992

Library of Congress Cataloging-in-Publication Data
Terts, Abram, 1925–
    [Kroshka TSores. English]
    Little Jinx / Abram Tertz ; translated by Larry P. Joseph and
Rachel May ; with a foreword by Edward J. Brown.
        p.   cm.
    Translation of: Kroshka TSores.
    ISBN 0-8101-1016-4 (alk. paper). — ISBN 0-8101-1041-5 (pbk. :
alk. paper)
    I. Title.
PG3476.S539K713   1992
891.73'44—dc20   91-45659
                                                            CIP

To Ernst
Theodor
Amadeus
Hoffman's
radiant memory

Contents

Foreword

"Abram Tertz" appeared in the West in 1959 as the pseudony-
mous author of an essay written in the Soviet Union entitled
"What Is Socialist Realism?" The essay was an ironical and
irreverent treatment of official Soviet literature and the canon
under which it was produced. Instead of a "realism" that gave
a false account of Soviet reality, Tertz espoused a style for
Soviet literature more suited to its subject matter and more in
tune with the modern world, a style featuring the absurd and
the fantastic. With the help of a French student in Moscow,
he was able to smuggle out of the Soviet Union and publish
in the West that essay together with a number of fictions
called "Fantastic Tales." The stories featured a "phan-
tasmagoric art" full of paradox and puzzles, and often enough
couched in an idiom, to put it mildly and modestly, quite free
of the puritanical shackles of the Soviet printed page. In fact,
the whole performance of this "Tertz" was by Soviet stan-
dards scandalous, if not indeed criminal, and his true identity
became a matter not only for literary critics to speculate upon
but for the KGB to investigate and expose.

The Soviet writer behind the pseudonym was indeed exposed in 1965 as a very able and usually publishable literary
critic and research scholar of the Institute for World Litera-

ture (IMLI), Andrei Donatovich Sinyavsky (b. 1925), who had written excellent studies of Gorky, Akhmatova, Babel, and many others. There were things in his list of published writings which might have alerted the doltish authorities to the fact that he was different, *very* good, even idiosyncratic: for instance, he had written a brilliant introduction to the Poets' Library edition of the poetry of Pasternak, which appeared in Moscow in 1965, and even earlier he had coauthored (with Ivan Golomshtok) a study of the art of Picasso (1960). But on the whole the quiet Soviet scholar Andrei Sinyavsky remained, as he himself once put it, "an honest intellectual, inclined to compromises and to an isolated and contemplative life." Yet he harbored within himself an alter ego who brooked no compromises, "the impudent, fantastic, Abram Tertz." And Tertz got him into big trouble.

Sinyavsky was arrested in 1965 and, after a black farce of a trial in which scenes torn out of context from his fictions were used to prove an intent to slander the Soviet Union, he was sentenced to seven years of hard labor. The violent absurdity of the trial was protested publicly in a statement signed by a number of Soviet writers and critics, and the whole process created among Soviet intellectuals a physical revulsion which they can still taste as they remember it. But the sentence was carried out, and Sinyavsky was dispatched to a prison camp in Potma.

He was released in 1971 after five years, with time off for something, probably not good behavior. He obtained permission to emigrate in 1973 and settled in Paris, where he teaches Russian literature at the Sorbonne.

Little Jinx is one of a number of Sinyavsky's postexile works that bear the name of his alter ego, Abram Tertz, as author. This brief, heavily laden story of alienation, rejection, and absolutely blameless guilt is one of the greatest products of Sinyavsky/Tertz's perverse and tender art, and I venture the opinion that it is indeed a great and memorable work. It has been compared with his earlier and similarly poignant story "Pkhentz," where the central character is an accidental visitor to Earth from a planet in a distant galaxy, a creature endowed with a beautifully exfoliated plantlike body whose rich profusion of arms and eyes must be constricted into an ugly humpbacked shape in order to pass among us as human. The theme of an individual human essence, a soul, or something, encased and cramped in an ungainly and ugly integument—its "body"—is deep and recurrent in Sinyavsky. The "little jinx" Sinyavsky of this story is burdened with a dwarfish and repellent exterior that separates him from "normal" humanity. One of the entries in a set of aphorisms Tertz published under the title "Random Thoughts" points to this human problem: "What is the body? A kind of outer envelope, a diving suit. And it could be that I, sitting in my diving suit, just keep wriggling and coiling."

The title in Russian of the story here translated "Little Jinx" is "Kroshka Tsores," a combination of the Russian word for "a tiny thing" and the Hebrew word for grief or sorrow. The English translation chosen here gives emphasis to the little sorrow-bringer's conviction, one shared by his mother and his dog among others, that his very presence brings misfortune. This is the tale of how poor Sinyavsky, though wishing his five half-brothers well, had a part in and felt responsible for the deaths of each one in turn. While the author on the title page is given as Tertz, the central character is named Sinyavsky, and thus the writer's pseudonym and alter ego has given us the terribly poignant story of a Soviet writer, that little sorrow, little misfit, Andrei Sinyavsky. It goes without saying that the story is not in any literal or obvious sense autobiographical, but the position and fate of the central character—a compulsive writer—surely alludes to a personal pain. The character Sinyavsky acquired a stutter as a child, which he thinks was cured by a fairy pediatrician, but he nonetheless continues to speak, and especially to write, with an impediment. He is rewarded as a student for producing conventional claptrap on third-rate Soviet authors and on trite Soviet topics, and he is consistently a loyal supporter of the Soviet way of life, once praising the collective farm where his brother was an agronomist, in awkward but rosy formulas: "You really have a nook of the future here. It's a veritable Thomas More's Utopia! As soon as Stalin finds out, you'll have a medal on your chest! The Order of the Fighting Red Flag!" And he goes on, even in spite of his brother's negative comment on the system—a remark for which he is sent to exile and death—to develop his ungainly dithyramb: "However, the farm air, as it seemed to me, was drunk with calm and well-being. It smelled like honey. Fresh hay. Dragonflies soared by. The grass was crackling with springing grasshoppers, which pawed the air whenever they fell over, trying to get back up on their horses' legs. The sun was scorching. O summer! O childhood! O quiet pleasures for their own sakes!"

Little Sinyavsky's linguistic lapses, which sometimes verge

on linguistic "hooliganism" (in the words of the real Sinyavsky), include mistakes in diction, various solecisms, errors in syntax and agreement, and occasional efforts at clumsily elevated poetic statement. Such a style has taxed the considerable ingenuity of the translators, who have produced—miraculously it seems to me—a text that not only transmits the skillfully calculated lameness of the linguistic vehicle carrying the story, but at the same time, as does the Russian text itself, fully communicates the agonizing experience of total rejection and utter aloneness, along with feelings of guiltless guilt before humanity itself for the world's suffering and evil. No human being who reads it can escape some involvement with "little Sinyavsky."

A Note on the Translation

The translation offered here was begun as part of the work in a translation seminar offered in the Department of Slavic Languages at Stanford University. The original participants, in addition to Larry P. Joseph and Rachel May, were Mary Lucia Bun and Henry Pickford, who made a substantial contribution to the early drafts of the translation but were obliged to withdraw from the final stages. The subtle problems of translation that developed made it necessary to consult with many literary and linguistic experts. Our prime consultant was Andrei Sinyavsky himself, who taught at Stanford during the spring of 1987. Many others have helped with advice on difficult problems, and among them we should mention Lazar Fleishman and Gregory Freidin, whose native control of idiom and background we exploited freely, and

Vera Dunham, whose graceful mastery of both English and Russian we occasionally had at our disposal. Lazar Fleishman should be given additional and generous credit for assistance at critical moments in practical matters of contact and communication.

Of course, none of the shortcomings of this version are to be blamed on any consultant, least of all Sinyavsky (the real one). The translators and I take full responsibility and credit, if there is any, for the text before you.

Edward J. Brown

Translators' Preface

It feels slightly odd that what started out as the collaborative effort of five people now has only two names attached to it. Henry Pickford and Mary Lucia Bun contributed first drafts of several chapters, and they and Edward J. Brown had so much to say about each turn of phrase, each difficult choice that it is hard to sort out at this point whose words are whose. Our debt to all of them lies deeper than simple choice of words: in the lively, sometimes heated discussions of each draft we learned more about language, literature, and the beautiful complexity of the act of translating than any of us might have expected. We also owe many thanks to Lazar Fleishman, for insights into Tertz's language, and especially to Andrei Donatovich for helping us explore his words.

The foreword explains some of the specific textual difficulties we encountered, and we will leave the innumerable others to the reader's imagination. The issue of the title deserves further mention, however. As Edward J. Brown has pointed out, "Kroshka Tsores" means "Little Tsuris," from the Yiddish word for sorrow or woe. By changing it to "Little Jinx" we eliminate several layers of allusion, all in the interest of accessibility. First, we regretfully abandon the Yiddish element, which suggests in the Russian that one reason the hero is such a misfit may be that he is Jewish. This suggestion resonates with the fact that Sinyavsky himself, who is not Jewish, chose a Jewish pseudonym for his own artistic alter ego, Abram Tertz. An equally significant reference in the original title is to an E. T. A. Hoffmann story, *Klein Zaches genannt Zinnober,* the very popular Russian translation of which is called *Kroshka Tsakhes*. This is a story of a repulsive, mumbling nitwit who receives a fairy's blessing early in life, as a result of which he gains credit for the virtues of those around him. At the expense of the truly gifted and virtuous, he eventually becomes the darling—and the embarrass-ment—of high society, until he is magically exposed. Like the Yiddish meaning of *tsuris,* this is a reference that would be far more obvious to Russian readers, who are perhaps Hoffmann's most devoted fans, than to their Anglophone counterparts.

Finally, we wish to dedicate this translation to the memory of a most delightful and inspiring man, Edward J. Brown, whose imprint is everywhere in this book and in our hearts as well.

Little Jinx

I

I was born and raised a completely normal child. True, as my mother rocked me off to sleep in my incredibly squeaky crib, she did have to keep hushing me, "Rest, rest your head, my little heartache." In the adjoining room of our communal apartment, old Polina Mikhailovna Glinka had long been dying a painful death, and my mother tried to drown out the groans of the half-crazy alcoholic with the cradle's creaking. The old woman already had bedsores, and the Kuznetsov brothers, on the lookout for their chance of getting her private room, were playing the role of her caretakers by turning her from side to side in the evenings. This made her scream something awful, and the entire apartment building was up in arms. As a result, around the age of four I began to stutter, and there was soon nothing I could do to control the spasms in my vocal cords. I would talk something like this: "M-m-mom, I w-w-want s-s-ome m-m-milk!"

And so I began to beg for mercy. Started begging for mercy at about age five. I began to cry out to the Lord in my thoughts because, having lost all faith, I had forgotten how to speak. And I "said," if my words could be made printable and readable: "Mama," I said, "send me a good fairy from heaven with the power to make wishes come true. I beg you with all my might. A fairy! I need a fairy immediately!"

It was as if I knew in advance that wishes do come true sooner or later, if you wish hard enough. My mother could not make heads or tails of why I was giving her such a hard time.

Then Dora Aleksandrovna, the pediatrician, came. "What are you crying for, little fella?" she inquired brightly, patting me on the tummy and examining my throat with a forehead lamp and a cold, chrome-plated spoon that made me gag. I recall that her handbag, at the head of the bed, smelled of perfume.

"F-f-f-airy!" I spluttered. She laughed. I was barely five and she *laughed* at my infelicitous salutation. And she pulled her perfumed purse toward her. When she opened it, I could see the colorful bills and thick packets of money inside. At that moment it seemed she had everything to offer. Fame. Fortune. Power. And if you want, even Dora Aleksandrovna herself, together with her cute little handbag, which she frugally snapped shut—just in case.

"What do you want, young man?"

Owing to my illness and tender age, I got hung up on poetry. I dreamt of nothing more than that my speech should resound and flow unimpeded, winging from my lips in perfect octaves. Life as seen through my backward conceptions of the time took refuge exclusively in the unattainable freedom and ease of pronouncing appropriate tirades on any given topic. I'd be rambling on and then suddenly I might toss in: "Voroshilov's on his horse / Everything is right on course."

Voroshilov, so they say, rode out on horseback every evening from his mansion into the side streets of the Arbat, by himself without a guard, to take the air on his evening constitutional. And everything was indeed right on course. Hooves clattered. Moscow serenely slept. But I simply could not get that memorable little rhyme out right. If only I had been granted the flair and talent of an orator, a writer, or a fabulist, what stories I could have told! . . .

"H-h-ave it y-y-our way, young m-m-an."

Dora Aleksandrovna was disappointed. A smile darted across her blanched lips.

"H-h-how are you g-g-oing to p-p-ay?"

"However you like, Good Fairy!"

"W-w-ith l-l-l. . . ."

"With love? Sure!"

Since I didn't know what love was, I relinquished it gladly. I waived my right to goodness, fame, and fortune. Everything beautiful in the world. That is how, without having an inkling of what I was doing, I sold myself to the devil. But in exchange, I began to talk. My tongue came untied. From the moment Dora Aleksandrovna left, my stutter vanished.

2

I graduated from high school, thanks to my tongue, with distinction. My essays, "The Image of Russian Woman in Nekrasov's Epic Poem 'Red-Nosed Frost'" and "Why We Like Ilya Isakovsky," made quite a sensation and won an award in the House of Pioneers. For one about Staimyl Studenbekov I received a certificate from the regional committee of the Komsomol. I need hardly mention that I was a great aficionado of Staimyl Studenbekov. . . .

My other qualities, however, did not endear me to my fellow students. They shunned me. The teachers tyrannized over me for my unclean shoes, hair, and nails. But I—I know that it was not my nails that were at issue: no one in the class was more fastidious than I. It was just that something in my humble shape was not to their liking. Bow-legged, short-statured, an "eternally brooding expression on my brow"—in their eyes I was something like Lermontov's Demon. I learned a lot about life from poems. For example:

And so, she was called Tatiana. . . .

How beautifully expressed! If called on in class, I had only to open my mouth and everyone would be amazed at how smoothly my tongue moved in parallel.

I am pretty much a melancholy sort. But just say something or write something, and tomorrow all the seas and oceans will bow down at our feet. I could build a new city in two paragraphs. Ah, fairy-witch, you did not give me horns for nothing! If worse comes to worst, I'll migrate into a manuscript. I am far more attractive on paper. There I will arouse no one's suspicions. There, on paper, I am pure in people's eyes. We might as well become a hermit and spin silent yarns with the spines of the books in the cabinet. We'll live by day, write by night. All real things were and are written at night. Even when it is broad, broad daylight outside. . . .

Sometimes in the evening I remember Dora Aleksandrovna: "Where are you, my little button? Come to me! . . ."

I refused to believe that as I was growing up she was growing older. She wasn't that sort of person. . . .

Once I found myself noticing that the water flowed from the faucet in convoluted spirals, like a screw, just as the bronze faucet, sticking up above the sink, forced itself into my consciousness, while the brief pipe, eaten by corrosion, gave a stern outflow and nuance to everything that passed. How much water flowed while I washed! But the sink still looked the same, like a plodding abstractionist's squelched bravado. . . .

"Isn't that all just pure aesthetics?" I ask myself, with some confusion. "Aren't you overlooking objective reality?" And I answer myself, "No, it is not aesthetics. Water really does flow in ornate twists, and you must account for that. Not just for the surface, but for the ardor and the intention of impassioned things and phenomena. 'Artistic' applies not only to the way flowers bloom but to the way they wither and rot, and to the way the sink turns green and moldy and the radiator wheezes. To put it crudely, nothing unartistic exists at all."

With this impression fresh in my mind I rush off to the university. By now I am studying at Moscow State University (MGU, in scientific lingo). I stop in at the assembly ground at the Commauditorium and—what a sight! My department-mates are standing around conferring about something. I push my way in unsolicited.

"Well met, guys," I say. Zero response. I have grown accustomed to the general coldness but have tried not to succumb to it. After all, they wouldn't take up pen or word to argue with me. By this time I am extremely well-read. I'm a smooth talker. I can tackle them at any level.

"Is that you, Little Jinx?" responds Alik Zweiback, who was also a bit on the lame side but who got along with me. A well-grounded fellow. He could slash Blok and Gumilev to ribbons—with citations. "Giving rise to an organ out of the sixth sense," as I recall it now. . . .

I must explain something: I am a dwarf. Not in the fullest sense of the word, of course, but I am, to put it another way, short, shorter than average. It's unbearable to have to push my way into the middle of a crowd. Thanks to Zweiback I make headway.

And what do I hear? Holy Venus de Milo! It's a conversation about dogs! These students are involved in the most heartwarming discussion. To arms! Someone praises German shepherds, despite our victory over Germany; someone else takes up the cause of the fox terrier; and another, taking the bit between his teeth, extols above all the Doberman pinscher, of all things. Absolute freedom of speech—just like in Hyde Park. And there is not a single Cosmopolite among us. . . . Here we stand, all pals together, discussing dogs as freely as if we were in Olde England. . . .

"Friends," I say, butting my way into the conversation, "let me direct your attention to the honorable dachshund, which you seem to have omitted. Or have you forgotten it? Perhaps you've never seen one? Then listen to me—I know the dachshund. An artistic animal: short, with crooked legs. But it does have an objective existence, which must be taken into account. It is as graceful as a lizard, as insinuating as a snake, but kind and—and serene. How can I describe it to you? Perhaps you can call to mind a little Louis XVI table in the rococo style, with curved legs? . . ."

I simply cannot imagine what possessed me to get involved in their conversation. I had had almost nothing to do with any of them for half a year. And now, "How d'ye do?—A dachshund!"

A profound and uncomfortable silence descended on the group. No one looked in my direction, as if I had put my foot in my mouth. But was there really anything so negative in what I had said? Decide for yourselves. Is there any reason why I shouldn't have let bygones be bygones and joined in their conversation—even if it was only about dogs—on equal terms with them, like brothers? It is as if even the words that were my gift from God were cursed for all time on my eloquent lips. . . .

Dora (this one, too, was named Dora) hung her head. Her

sweet little face grew sad. Agitation probably was forcing her to struggle against her slight, crumpled speech defect—not at all a serious one, I assure you; in fact, it only made her more attractive, like a birthmark on the little cheek I so wanted to kiss. Sometimes the very register of a woman's voice suggests tenderness, and that deceives us. . . . Like a piano, or a harp. . . . So Dora pronounced these words, stretching out the musical phrase like something incredibly elevated: "Sinyavsky, you always have something vile on your mind! You are always cooking something up, always spinning out the strangest things. You chose that breed on purpose because it's unnatural—and decadent—and deformed—on short little legs! . . ."

She was almost in tears.

"Why, he's a dachshund himself!" barked Mikhailov, a giant who had been pursuing Dora—and not in vain, as it turned out. A real lout. A bear. He would beat the shit out of anyone who asked for it, and even anyone who didn't—he liked nothing better. Among the university crowd he was considered very attractive, but he wasn't exactly a Lomonosov in the intellectual department. I, for one, could pin him to the mat and make an ass of him with no trouble at all. This time, however, Mikhailov took his revenge.

"He's a dachshund himself!"

At this they all began to sound off, to bleat, with vengeance in their hearts. "Death to Sinyavsky!" squealed Alik Zweiback. And Dora, her eyelashes glittering, sent her chosen one a glance laden with promises. The company dispersed, as if I had mortally offended them all. Even Alik, who previously would have given me the benefit of the doubt, had his say. On his way out he said, without looking at me:

10

"Look, Sinyavsky, you're right, in principle, about your dachshund, but this time you've gone too far. I can no longer speak to you, not until you make a public apology to everyone. . . ."

They all dispersed somewhere, leaving me alone with my thoughts of Dora. . . .

It can't be said that there was nothing between us. She understood plainly that I liked her, and she made use of my services for her coursework, when no one was looking. One semester I was even seized with a passion for writing verses, which I kept hidden. I'll print them here, at the end of the road—let them be read later on:

> . . . I loved you then with all my soul,
> Holding you often in my arms!

The images came out a bit overblown. But that's the sort of thing that is beyond our control—like our body temperature. And besides, how can you compare literature and reality? Everything's backwards. Like dregs in a barrel, you swirl aimlessly, agonizing over some single idea that you have not yet licked clean. You finger the ball bearings in your head until they take shape of their own accord. Just remember, your every word must be a nail, pounded right through! . . .

Life, meanwhile, flowed drably on. Every single person had something except me, standing alone in the desert like Pushkin's terrible, poisonous "Upas tree." Once I could not resist asking, "What is it you have in common with that dolt Mikhailov, Dora?"

That is not, incidentally, how I began the conversation, but how I did begin is of little importance right now.

"Lay off, Sinyavsky," she answered with a smile that suggested she had long since been expecting my comment. "What do we have in common? Nothing. Well, if you must know, I did sleep with him three times. But who's counting? . . ."

"What? What did you say? 'Slept with him'? How vulgar, Dora! How degrading! . . ."

I grasped her suddenly by the hand.

"Hey, Sinyavsky, be a pal, don't touch me! Your fingers, they're like a frog's. All sticky, sort of, and repulsive. So Mikhailov's got your goat? Well, I only slept with him once, so calm down! . . ."

But I could not calm down. I already knew that this was going to be my wretched lot. A woman, like a dog, can sense a dead loser, and she will always cling to a winner. After all, I couldn't hang around her feet like ballast, could I? I avoided meeting her and only followed her with my eyes from a distance and dreamed. . . .

> You are my idol:
> I worship you from afar.
> You don't notice my "I,"
> My world is very hard.

The business with the dachshund wasn't finished with me yet. . . .

Soon after that Dora left the department; rumor had it that she had gotten married to Mikhailov. They said she was unhappily married. I don't know; I didn't poke my nose into her business. One thing is certain, though: in his place I would have made a goddess of her, my Dora. . . .

At some point (I had finished university by then) we ran into each other in a grocery store, standing in line for milk. She was probably in her eighth month, and I took an interest.

"How are you, Dora? May I congratulate you? . . ."

I have noticed in pregnant women that their facial beauty and physical self-awareness move toward the center, to what lies growing and maturing within them for the future. The same is true of great thinkers, immersed in hypotheses about themselves from which they cannot possibly be reeled back into life. They are all profoundly concentrated somewhere in their stomachs. But to my great amazement, her ashen cheeks suddenly blushed and her dulled eyes flared.

"Oh, my little sorrow, Little Jinx!" The words escaped her lips with that suggestion of contempt that is so wounding when it concerns the distant past and an irreparable mistake. "You were sound asleep the whole time! What a girl you let slip by; when she was coming on to you, too. And now look at us. . . ."

She pointed to her big stomach with malice, as though I were to blame.

"'Coming on,' Dora? When? Where? . . ."

"Don't you remember the conversation about dogs? I was counting on you so much. Couldn't you guess? Oh, Sinyavsky, Sinyavsky. . . ."

"But Dora, you hinted yourself that you had something going with Mikhailov. . . ."

"And you believed me? You were glad? I was only teasing you a little. Playing the coquette, to arouse your jealousy and create a rivalry. . . . Maybe I thought you'd wise up. . . . But why recall that now? Two liters, please!"

She sealed her milk can with a clang on the marble counter. During our quiet squabble the line had moved forward. I stood stunned, forgetting the milk and staring at Dora. My heart rolled over inside me like an infant in its mother's womb. Never think you are worse off than the rest. There will always be someone who is even worse off. We are all flapping our tails, more or less, like fish on ice. . . .

"Wake up, citizen!" snapped the saleswoman, grabbing the glass jar right out of my hand. I got one liter. But Dora had already moved on with her full milk can, not waiting for mine to be filled. The crowd gave way before her indignant stomach. There was no point in my running after her with explanations. Besides, how could I chase after her with my milk jar full to the brim? . . .

3

It did not become clear right away that I was the cause of other people's misfortunes. But if I just sketch out a diagram of the things that, because of me, befell my brothers one by one, as if by a script, you will see. It's a shame, as they say, but it's a fact.

My mother had five sons from her first marriage, each more successful than the last. But I, the sixth and youngest, never knew my father and lived with my mother as a castoff, oblivious to the family troubles. My brothers, every one of them a fine fellow, had scattered around the country. I saw them only on the rare occasions when our paths crossed, and I judged their successes by the colorful stories told by my mother, who was growing more and more distant from me as time passed.

Let us start with the youngest, Nikolai, who, by the way, had graduated as a navigator and been appointed the captain of a seining ship when I was barely seven. At the time of his promotion in the spring, we were vacationing at the beach in Sochi, and my brother, to celebrate his appointment, threw a party on board the ship that had been put in his care, dragging my mother along, and even me. I will not go into the beauties of the Black Sea here, but when we moored we picked up a puppy to which I became attached, and while the adults drank champagne, I played with him to the sounds of a waltz on deck. My brother, who was setting sail the next day, came out on deck to cool off and undertook to make a sailor of my poor Gurgle (that was the name I later gave my little dog, in secret), by tossing him toward Sochi and the whims of fate. Swinging him by the legs like a hare, he flung him overboard and seemed carried away by the pleasure of launching his cherished star.

"I," says he, "will make a sea wolf out of him!"

Gurgle disappeared, squealing, into the deep, and when he came sputtering to the surface after drinking his fill, I wasn't about to wait for him to drown but jumped in like a little soldier to the rescue of my comrade, as I had been taught to do. I swim pretty well, and everything would have come off all right if the girl, whose name has slipped my mind, the captain's fiancée and an excellent swimmer, had not leapt into the sea after us, dressed just as she was and crying, "Save him! Save him!" Our Nikolai completely lost his head, probably already reading his shame in the eyes of his fiancée. He throws off his tunic, takes a running start, and—splash!—in he goes, like a swallow in pursuit, in perfect stunt-pilot form, as everyone later confirmed.

In the end, they fished Gurgle out, and I too escaped with nothing but a slight shock. The fiancée, laughing and triumphant, climbed up on the deck, looking like a mermaid in her soaked dress. The only one who didn't emerge was my brother, the captain. His leap had taken him exceptionally deep and he had split his skull on the anchor.

It was at that point that my mother, wringing her hands,

pronounced for the first time: "You are to blame for everything! You killed your brother!"

True, she never repeated this quite so literally. But the words had been spoken and branded me for life. . . .

Ever since then, whatever I do is always bad. It turns out, in the final analysis, that you are to blame for everything. Oh Little Jinx, Little Jinx! How I grieve for you! After all, you probably just wanted to be good and useful, like everyone else. But what on earth have you done? Why have you brought with you so much misery? . . .

Or perhaps at some point—long, long ago—we shamelessly committed a sin? And we ourselves don't even understand how much we are to blame. Were we not evil and guilty, neither Hitler nor Stalin could have surfaced from among us. There would be no death. "Look back in anger!" said the nameless author. And I repeat after him, Look back in anger, and you will look back at yourself! . . .

My second brother we also lost suddenly, but in a somewhat different way. It happened two years later, but again with my indirect and involuntary complicity. He worked as an agronomist at "Daybreak," a leading collective farm, and he invited my mother to spend a month in the country. Me, a brainless nine-year-old suckling pig, he dragged with him everywhere he went—all around the fields and the vegetable gardens. He took me to the poultry farm, where he had a real incubator set up to hatch chickens. The year was '38, and the country, with my brother's help among the rest, was flourishing. Wanting to say something nice, I marveled at the apiary, where Ol' Man Kostya, the limping bee-master, had just lavished me with comb honey.

"You really have a nook of the future here. It's a veritable Thomas More's Utopia! As soon as Stalin finds out, you'll have a medal on your chest! The Order of the Fighting Red Flag, Pavel! . . ."

He suddenly started swearing in an unfamiliar language that made me feel sick.

"Ha, you miserable onion tears! What do you know? And what's a worker's day-wage worth anyway? Zilch point zero. . . ."

I wasn't about to argue; those day-wages tripped me up. However, the farm air, as it seemed to me, was drunk with calm and well-being. It smelled like honey. Fresh hay. Dragonflies soared by. The grass was crackling with springing grasshoppers, which pawed the air whenever they fell over, trying to get back up on their horses' legs. The sun was scorching. O summer! O childhood! O quiet pleasures for their own sakes!

In the mornings a little bird used to dive into our front garden and let out an unforgettable trill: "Whippoorwill! Whippoorwill!" I've never come across a purer or more blissful sound. Lifetimes have gone by since the days of that little bird. But I believe it still sings in that great wildlife preserve in the sky! . . .

We would never even have remembered the ill-starred episode in the bee garden if my brother had not been taken away from us in the beginning of August, upon his denunciation by Ol' Man Kostya, who had heard everything perfectly from his hut. They even took me in, on a police motorcycle. They stuffed me with pastries, promised me a watch to boot and a fountain pen with a rust-resistant shaft, trying to dig out what Pavel and I had personally plotted against Stalin and the details of how we were planning to sabotage the economy. I cried, I swore an oath, and, in a face-to-face confrontation with Ol' Man Kostya, I even denied the curses that Pavel had supposedly been unable to resist uttering in a fit of temper. All in vain!

"Sinyavsky, if you were just four little years older," the interrogator said to provoke me, "you'd be off to swing a miner's hack with your brother. The little apple does not fall far from the apple tree. You and your mother had better make yourselves scarce. Go far away. Get going! . . ."

And we did. My mother lamented constantly that I had made Pavel utter kulak propaganda with my inappropriate chatter. But the thought had never entered my mind. How could I have injured anyone, if I harbored in my soul neither dagger nor venom? Helpless and confined, like a little toe, what did I know about politics? But the scales had fallen from my eyes. It turned out that even the lofty right to spout off about anything that pops into your head—a right won with blood—carries with it something insidious and contrary. For that purpose it would certainly be a better idea to treat myself to a spiral notebook for jotting down noteworthy items. Perhaps someday, as I pore over this notebook, I will cheer up and come to my senses. . . .

And thus Pavel left the scene, and twenty years later, during the rehabilitation, he was nowhere to be found. He disappeared somewhere in Vorkuta, from arrhythmia of the heart. . . .

. . . It's cold, goddammit! The lights should be on. It's warmer with the lights on. But I just lie here and listen to the automobiles speeding by. Are you there, dog? It's good that you're here. She's curled up in the dark, under the armchair or like a rug by the door, gnawing away at something by herself. Now she's asleep—and gnawing again, in her sleep. Still, how a dog adorns one's existence! You get up, and it wags its tail. It starts dancing or turning somersaults. Without any tom-foolery, it brings you the shoe that you lost last night. Or the sock you dropped behind the radiator. . . .

Another eighteen-wheeler just rumbled by. Hearing it move off, never to return, I send my unspoken blessing after it. But what a burden I must be for others! Even for this heavy, matutinal eighteen-wheeler. . . .

No, thank God, it's still night. But how am I to overcome it, shifting to the next page, to the next day, which I don't even want to remember? Must I go through it again from the beginning? What's it to you? You're just reading! But I'm the one who's responsible, as we shift into tomorrow. Stay, night; wait a little: it's already morning! Night, and already morn-ing. . . .

If only I could sink into sleep, so as not to experience the superfluous. You fall asleep without even getting warm, and you keep recalling in your sleep that your toes still haven't thawed out. . . . If only you could get some kind of anaes-thetizing injection!

I go to bed with one thought—to collapse onto the mat-tress as soon as possible. But it seems as though the darkness in the room is the shadows of those who have died, all ema-nating from me. A blind sun, giving off nocturnal rays that offer no warmth. How many have died on our account! And we drag on, we keep trying, carrying the invisible weight of those departed creatures that have been dumped into our memories, emanating still. It's no simple matter!

The room smells of dog; there's a touch, as we say, of mutt in the air, and it calms me: it's home. There's nothing nicer, I must confess, than the damp smell of dog. Damp, as after a rain, a light autumn drizzle, when it's dark and dank all around you, but the smell warms and intoxicates you, forming an almost tactile hallucination. Question: When this comes over me, where does it come from? Is it a hint about my father, about my infancy? And where's the dog?

After my mother's demise, I made inquiries among our former apartment-mates. I asked around the courtyard and at the Housing Office. I asked the old—even pre-revolutionary—scattered sands. I never did find out who my father was and what had happened to him. Not even how old I was. One thing is certain: Just before he went—whether he died or just left suddenly—his dog stopped coming to him for exactly one month. Before that she had been devoted like no one else; she never left his side. But no matter how tenderly he called her, she would wag her tail at the voice and look away. She would hide under the table or bed, cower in the corner, or press close to the landlady's legs. The landlady was by nature indifferent to animals, but she kept this dog in the house, albeit reluctantly, as a concession to my father. In short, the dog was manifesting a strange hostility toward him. Somehow, smelling the evil that lay behind him, she avoided and feared him. (It seems, by the way, that without him she soon perished.) I never did find either my father or the dog. Of course, it's possible that I did not even exist at the time they both disappeared.

Somehow I am brought up short by my father every time. I keep moving along, then I stumble. It would be easier for me if I just had the slightest inkling about my father. Anything, I think, even that he was a horrible debauchee, a drunkard, a thief, an enemy of the people. Yes, even the devil himself. At least then it would be clear where my roots lie. But the devil isn't here and—I am. Children undoubtedly do turn up who are born into sin, who give off a mysterious evil that spreads across the land, making everyone respond with revulsion. I am of their numbers. Not a bad person, just—"Godforsaken, Devil take 'im." . . . But can it be that, with time, even I will be absolved of my spoonful of sins because I didn't hide anything, because I tried to write everything down? For some sentence or other, beautifully said, or for a stray, inadvertent line? . . .

Well, finally my feet got warm and I fell asleep, conscious that what would be left of me the next day on the bed would be many helpless little pages leading nowhere. . . . My glasses were pressing into my forehead, but I was beside myself and in my sleep noted down blindly that soon it would be morning and the night was slipping away, slipping out from under my feet. I am tormented and fettered by the remaining minutes of freedom. After them, at the slightest dawning of the light, I won't be able—I won't have the right—to say one more word, like a ghost that suddenly falls silent and collapses under a rock at cockcrow. But I am still living and I keep writing. . . .

About what? About how the trees in the courtyard have probably already darkened on the background of the paling skies, along which ink-cloud dirigibles float silently by, all in the same direction. A pipe stands, tall and slim, on the edges of the wall, like a suicide, ready to jump. A minute, a second more, and the birds will start to chirp. It seems that in my sleep I can already distinguish the first trial warbles. "Whip-poorwill!" It means they are off to work, and I—back to the graveyard. The next shift is coming on. It's their turn! The silhouette of my worn, sagging shoes stand out remotely against the floor, as if they were the dark feet of my severed legs. My shirt hangs on the armchair like a spineless, decapitated body. And the armchair has rolled up into the pose of a person sleeping curled up in an armchair. There is no dog. Won't make it in time. Asphalt. Run. It's getting light, and if something were to happen, your cry wouldn't reach them, they wouldn't hear your call. There's the empty, white street, and I myself am congealing into some kind of abstract sculpture on the corner. . . .

4

After Pavel's arrest we regained our grip on life with the help of my third brother, Vasily. His rank and duties as C.O. of a border post made all the difference. And soon enough, to our good fortune, the Great War broke out, bringing Vasily even greater distinction. And did it ever occur to me that I would lend a hand in his senseless death?! No, never. And yet, so it was. . . .

My brother was returning to the front from a special mission for the augmentation of reserves in the Urals, and since he had some spare leave, he dropped in at our evacuation site to see Mama and me on his way. It was a January night when he, now a colonel, burst into the doorway with two suitcases and an orderly, shaking the snow from his high fur hat, stomping his feet loudly, fearing no one—and we leapt up from our cots.

"So, you little runt, still alive and kicking?" roared Vasily, tossing me up to the ceiling despite my fourteen years. "Gotta eat more if you want to grow up big and strong! You can't expect something for nothing, y'know!"

All of us who stood there gaping at him felt his fiery spirit waft over us and throughout the hut, like the musk of a bear in the junipers. What a racket he made in the morning, clearing his throat over the sink and slapping himself on his shoulders and sides! He took up our whole half of the hut, so that the Jews from Gomel who shared our evacuation lodging were afraid of us for half a year afterward, and even thought twice about pilfering Mama's and my wood supply from the collective shed.

He was with us for practically no time at all, less than three days, with his cologne, his shoulder belt, and his holstered pistol, which I was forbidden to touch on any account. This wasn't counting the orderly, who was always either asleep on the stove or off chasing girls—he was all shoe polish and vodka, and laughing himself silly. We enjoyed my brother's company—but not for long.

Mama had left for a teachers' meeting—she taught Russian in the village—and I, as befits a senior in high school, was availing myself of the least pretext to skip classes and hang out in town, hiding under her protective wing, when, toward evening of the third day, a messenger from the town soviet on a mad charger ran me down, grabbed me by the cap, leaned over me, and thrust a telegram into my hand.

"Who's it for?" it occurred to me to bellow into the snowy uproar.

"The Colonel!" came back out of the dark. "The Colonel himself, and it's urgent! From town! . . ."

"Telephonogram for you, Vasily," I absently announced as I walked in. My brother was shaving, and when he finished he splashed himself with cologne.

"Read it to me!"

On a pale-blue receipt, scrawled with a scratchy, peasant-style quill pen, were four words, which I read:

"Report to headquarters immediately."

"Signed?" he asked gruffly.

"No signature," I read.

And so he immediately followed the order: he strapped on his pistol, pulled on his high fur hat, called out to his fellow, who was sleeping off last night's adventures on the brick stove, and gave me a peck on the cheek.

"Tell Mother they've summoned me back. Take care, and remember me well. . . ."

A person disappears like steam, like the smell of a cigarette in a railroad restroom. You walk in and—someone who was there just a moment ago has completely disappeared, already intangible, ephemeral. In the empty hut I sit alone by the kerosene lamp and breathe in everything that remains of us after we're gone: the smell of shoe polish, vodka, aftershave, of the clean, white, winter underwear of a colonel. . . . I keep turning the telegram over in my hand. On the other side of it, scribbled upside down, is written: "To Sinyavsky—School Principal." The principal himself? What in tarnation? . . .

No one had ever sent me a letter or even a postcard, let alone a telegram. So it is probably no wonder that I laughed aloud. "To Sinyavsky?!" It made me sound important, like Lev Tolstoy, or Panferov. . . .

Aha, I get it. The principal, a veteran wounded in action, must be imagining himself a commissar, so he likes to call the school his "headquarters," that's all. Have they all gone out of their minds, or what? Granted, I've been skipping school and spending too much time with Mama in the village. But my brother was visiting. A colonel. From the front. And besides, I was still making the honor roll. But what about Vasya? Were they calling him in too? "Report immediately. . . ." What did Vasya have to do with it? God knows, Vasya was no kid. What in hell did he care about the principal? He didn't even have my last name: his was from the first marriage, Likhosherst. All my brothers were Likhoshersts. Mama was too. . . .

All this slowly worked its way into my consciousness, turning to ice in my veins: the telegram—it was for Sinyavsky. But who was rushing off to the front, to his death?—Vasya Likhosherst! . . .

With Vasily around, Mama and I had been living for the first time in our lives with a real, honest-to-God man. He snored at night in harmony with the orderly. He snorted and shaved, reeked and rioted—filled up our whole half of the hut. It was all so nice. Why? Because, well, because he was my brother, the Colonel! For the first time I came to understand what widowhood meant, and why, when word came from the War Commission, the women would wail for their lost men and make a whole epic out of their personal lyric lament. At that time, there was a constant moan throughout the villages, but we just reveled away without a care in the world—and failed to save our Vasya. . . .

Howling madly, I tore out of the hut into snowdrifts that came up to my waist. But really, how in the world was I to catch up with Likhosherst, who had been whisked away on horseback at the stroke of a pen? I ran the twelve kilometers to the station, hoping that he would still be waiting for the train, and then another twenty-four to the new aerodrome. But the snow we had that winter—nothing could get through it: up to the sky like a wall, this high! And in my foolishness I lost my way in the snowstorm; groping my way along overland, I staggered into the aerodrome at noon trying to catch a plane that had left at midnight.

I've never been so exhausted. Circles kept closing in on me. And the plane just kept climbing and climbing, clambering up the steps of heaven, horribly, hopelessly droning on. Waist-deep in the snow, I was watching my brother's actions on a screen: he climbed out of the jolly manure cart and into a half-empty supply truck while I was still coming to my senses, and he left the truck for a bomber to fly him to the advance position even before I managed, stumbling and falling, to crawl into the train station. And on the very first day of his arrival at the front, my brother takes it upon himself to lead his decimated battalion into battle, brandishing his pistol through the snowdrifts, and on the very first day he dies a hero's death near Minsk, near Gomel, near Narva—always farther and farther to the west—and he keeps falling and falling into the snow, just as I had scripted it for him, waist-deep, as I was vainly running for his plane.

And, it seems, those reserve soldiers on leave might have postponed their departure and had another week or two to enjoy themselves, had it not been for my telegram. And he, Vasily Likhosherst, would still be with us, to the joy of everyone. If it weren't for me, Sinyavsky!

Of all the crimes, of all the murders that have been laid at my feet, this death is the one for which I assume full responsibility. Yes, I really did put my brother in front of that bullet. But you are always, always in such a hurry. . . .

We have now come to the limit, the fourth brother, and I pause in bewilderment. Was it truly my fate to destroy the fourth one too? No, after all the other tangles I did my best never to cross his path; I vowed not to, and accepted my fate. Besides, I was already an adult, and what did I have to lose? His name was Yakov, but you wanted to say it louder, with the patronymic, or even call him triumphantly "Dr. Likhosherst," just as everyone else did, both to his face and behind his back. He wasn't much to look at: all nerves. He had swollen white corneas with tiny wormholes in their centers, behind unbelievably thick glasses in American frames. On his thin lips played an eternally sardonic smile: "Redyard Kiplink," "Oskar Waild," "Verlaine," "Verlibre": he loved to jingle foreign currency. . . .

Personally, I didn't much like Yakov: always "I," "I," "I"— up on everything, number one in everything. Before he was thirty he had managed to go bald and marry three times, not counting the nurses and assistants he had at his beck and call, just as in the harem of "The Fountain of Bakhchisarai." Well, what do you expect? He was head surgeon at the Botkin Hospital! But what was really interesting was that here I was, a bastard, which was undoubtedly how I appeared growing up to his bespectacled eyes, and he harbored a secret penchant for me, or perhaps it was concealed curiosity. He was always trying to corner me into conversations on delicate topics, quizzing me on various recherché and, at the time, illegal books, which I didn't even want to hear about lest I should inadvertently wreak some new horror. Take that bait and who knows what rabbit hole we might fall down. My only link to him was that about once a month, on average, I would run down to the hospital to pick up a prescription for Validol from him when Mama's heart would start acting up again.

For some reason, however, he never asked how she was doing. His nonchalant frown meant, "It'll pass." It's not inconceivable that they had their own accounts to settle. That was none of my business. And to try to keep out of harm's way, I adopted the strategy of using a maximum of two words in our brief encounters: "Yes" and "No." This made things easier—no chance of being drawn into conversation. I'd just take the prescription and be on my way. He even began to tease me, calling me "Yes-or-No." . . .

"Welcome, Yes-or-No!" He would call from the stairs in his white smock, with a broad grin, as if he were sizing me up and drawing me out like a splinter, with his provocative tweezers.

"Nurse, let this young man through. After all, this Bedlam is no place for our discussions about how spake Zarathustra or about Grigory Skovoroda's thoughts on the nature of the soul, is it, Yes-or-No? Quickly, now—yes or no? . . ."

"No," I would answer, though I stayed out in the waiting room. It worried me that he would use the formal "you" while throwing in sarcastic remarks. It could be that somehow he, too, was afraid of me, and that's why he would spread it on a bit thick. Or maybe he simply wanted to figure out what kind of creature I was, and so he fumbled about and probed me with that technique peculiar to doctors.

"So, you're here for the Validol again?"

"Yes."

"And you won't drop in for a visit? I can squeeze you in between consultations, if you want. . . ."

"No."

"Always no. I get it. Exams, seminars, coursework. . . . What are you reading?"

"Staimyl Studenbekov." I enunciated as confidently as possible through my dry lips, trying not to waver.

"Staimyl? Studen-bekov? Who the hell is that? You'd do better to take a look at. . . . Why don't you try . . . ?"

And he began to recite a list of writers whose very names, although I didn't even know them, took my breath away and sent shivers up and down my spine. Oh no, it wasn't for myself that I shuddered, but for him. . . . And then Yakov the Tempter would try to entice me into watching an operation on some bizarre brain tumor or some fascinating cyst, on the pretext of my being a student intern, which of course was strictly against the rules and would have ended badly for him. Or, with a knowing wink, he would try to motion me into the anatomy lab. . . . It seemed as though his very eyes, behind those glasses, were swimming in chloroform. Then, in order to avoid the danger, I would quickly announce that it was time to go. . . .

But apparently his fate was written on my forehead. There I was, stricken unconscious with a severe case of peritonitis, when he, the best surgeon in the place, who had put the whole professoriate on its feet, took up the scalpel himself. The next day weeping nurses divulged to me in confidence that, for the first time in his life, Dr. Likhosherst's hands had trembled during an operation. He was afraid, it seemed, that I would die right on the operating table.

But it turned out that when they opened me up, there was nothing seriously wrong with me; Yakov had just drawn one card too many. They say that after coming out of the operating room, he threw his gloves down on the tile floor and demanded a cigarette and a glass of straight alcohol, although he had never smoked or touched liquor in his life. "Yes-or-No," "Yes-or-No," his lips kept whispering, and everyone thought that he still doubted his diagnosis. But I know, I know who he was arguing with, whom he was challenging—he who had never once had a real conversation with me. There, before all of Medicine, which forgot to give him Validol, Yakov sank heavily into a chair and died of a heart attack. He probably thought that I didn't pull through due to his medical negligence. I understand him.

5

Before moving on to the fifth brother, I need a moment to recover from some disconcerting thoughts from around the time just following my release from the hospital. That year Mama and I had a falling out. She didn't say it in so many words, but I could tell by her eyes that it was physically painful for her to have me around. Besides, I was studying my tail off in the public library in order to graduate and tried to show my face at home as little as possible so as not to traumatize her further by the very sight of me. And it just so happened that in our irrecoverable losses, she was becoming increasingly diverted from me by new concerns—those of a grandmother—which had arisen in the household of the eldest son, Vladimir. Vladimir's wonderful little twins, a little boy and girl, were getting bigger. To make a long story short, Mama announced that she would move in with them to take care of the grandchildren. I did not dispute her right to play nursemaid unto her grandkids and be a lickspittle unto her blessed firstborn, but what really came as a rude awakening was when Mama suddenly called me by my last name, and with an antagonistic and partisan note in her voice, too, as if I belonged, well, to a different family.

"You are not a kid any more, Sinyavsky. Have you no shame?

Go off and study by yourself. It'll be better that way for the both of us. . . ."

This was the first time she had spoken to me in such an official tone, as though she had broken off all family ties with me. At that moment, I could not contain myself and demanded point-blank to know who my father was. Up till then, I had politely skirted around that slippery issue by holding my tongue, somehow sensing that it would make her ill at ease. But now I was peeved. Among the Likhoshersts I was, according to my passport, the only Sinyavsky. How come? Why? Condemned to be left all alone at home, I felt I deserved to have it out once and for all.

"That's none of your business. That's not the kind of thing one asks about. Don't you have your workbook exercises to attend to? Well then, get writing and not another peep from you! And stay out of my sight! I've had it!"

But I held firm. I thought that the source of Mama's and my misfortune and discontent must lie concealed somewhere deep in the shadows of my provenance.

"You'll find out on my deathbed! Just you wait—it won't be long now!"

As if I *wanted* her to die. I blew up. It was obvious that she didn't care about me in the least anymore. In the end, we quarreled and parted mutually wounded. Mama categorically refused to let me sort the family's dirty laundry with her. When I was gone one day, the Likhoshersts' private chauffeur had come by to pick her up without bag or baggage, and when I got back from the library I found the house empty. On the dining-room table lay, just as always, a note. She requested with her maternal importunity that I not disturb

34

Volodya by phone and that I not drag a man of such governmental importance away from his busy schedule for no good reason. Would be dropping by. Money for gas and electricity, rent transfer order, dinner would be on table. Signed: "Mama" in her familiar, rounded hand. My last dinner with Mama. . . .

Over and over, I pursue my imaginary dialogue with her. What do I need Ol' Volodya for? (That's what I used to call my eldest brother—Ol' Volodya—not that it was expected of me, but it reassured me.) He was so far from my innermost interests and plans that he was completely inaccessible to me. I couldn't even quite remember what position he held. I did know it was some government job; but then I need his life story, if you'll pardon the expression, like a hole in the head. He would toss pennies into Mama's retirement fund, but that meant beans. He palmed off a refrigerator on her as a birthday present—to vaunt his ego. He was dumping the "expropriated materials" he had acquired on his trip to Africa on the heap to "boost the economy," but it didn't take much to figure out that he really just wanted a change of furniture. What do I care? I hope that refrigerator steamrolls right over him. Lousy driver! Basically, I think that automobiles are responsible for the current decline in the arts. Really now, when you're behind the wheel, are you aware of the soul of thy neighbor? Your attention is riveted to the speed, the high-performance handling, the carburetor. And to burning up those miles. No D.A. can stop him. . . . But refrigerators (let's try to be fair) during that period were a novelty. A museum piece. A reliquary.

In short, my perceptions of Ol' Volodya were formed primarily by amateur photographs and newspaper clippings that Mama kept in her drawer like some national treasure. I couldn't even make out his face. Just a regular Kubla Khan. With bootlike jaws and an onionlike nose, a stiff collar out of which he oozed like toothpaste, in accordance with Party task directives, with a somber, distant, and dull gaze lacking a glimmer of understanding beneath his regulation forehead. The sort of face they paint in official portraits instead of a communiqué—completely devoid of thought. . . .

So all in all he saw me maybe once or twice, and always in a rush; once at Mama's birthday party and once at Yakov's funeral service, at which he appeared from out of the blue of his own accord to hold vigil for our brother. It never even crossed his mind to take notice of the existence of an insect like me. That's not to say, though, that he couldn't have easily afforded to have us over sometime for dessert at his mansion. No skin off his back. There may have been others I would have liked to intimidate, but on no occasion, despite my desire to do so, did I ever pose a threat to Prince Vladimir. . . .

However, the longer my incarceration dragged on, the deeper the idea of my unspeakable fate wormed its way into my breast. I made a point, once again, of not venturing out of the house any more than was necessary in order not to cross paths, insofar as possible, with *mes semblables*. Even going places on the tram was already a great luxury for me. That's fair, for to whom have I brought even the slightest bit of good? To no one—ever. And the world would be better off without me—without my interloping, my secret complicity and commiseration, which acted as a venomous fang. Is this perhaps a preventive cure? A guilt-vaccine for humanity, a humankind that knows only that it is trying to vindicate itself? Say what you will, but we all aspire to be vindicated—through work, through children, through books. But when you take a look at man at the end, just before death, he is left with nothing but the fear in his heart and the solitary hope for forgiveness—for he hath sinned. . . .

We make rationalizations, we really make an effort, but the evil wrought by us is ever growing. Wouldn't it be preferable to admit one's guilt from the very start? To state squarely, staring Truth straight in the face, "I have never met a person worse than me." Will not there then appear, like a lighthouse, the long-sought-after sin in salvation at which we sneered so? Will not the ascension into the light then begin? Now I say, cast the first stone at me: the refitting of society must begin with oneself. So I shall begin to retailor myself, offering to all of humanity a contagious pattern. It's easier to relate to oneself. More comfortable. Safer. You at least know who you are and why. "Where am I from?" I query. "Who am I? Of what am I guilty?" But perhaps I am not worse, but better than the rest. Then I think, in self-deprecation, "But just the same, I am a terribly good person and awfully intelligent. . . . How does the Lord still manage to tolerate me on Earth? And even if I am not universally liked, perhaps at least I find grace before Him alone?" No, people like me should be run over. . . .

As you can see, pangs of conscience tormented me but little. Most likely conscience has such a property. It also adapts itself to our physical and mental state and to our piddling position in society. There is nothing on earth we can't turn to our advantage. . . .

But something else did torment me: the hopelessness of my

predicament. Fine, to hell with them, with my brothers, whose paths I crossed like a black cat. But I didn't mean for it to happen! That which is wrought of us goes sliding back into the past and, shaping itself into a grim confession, proffers the reassurance that the past will not return. If it were the other way around, we would simply not be able to endure the cumulative injustices. They would burn us up alive. But, tell me, what am I supposed to do if it is known, not with hindsight, but with foresight, that every act I perform, everything I compose or think, will be wrong or backwards. And then they will expose and indict me! Would this work in favor of a writing career like mine, destroying a sense of progress? That may very well be the only reason that I do write—a move calculated so that I will keep crossing someone's path over and over. Fine. But how do you expect me to go on living when I myself realize that it would be best not to cross the path of a creature like me? I even empathize with Mama: she's not responsible for my coming out wrong.

I remember in my early childhood that there was only one kid in pioneer camp my age who was drawn to spend time with me, and in better than no time somehow Vadim and I became fast friends, bonding into a spiritual commonality. We read together and played ball. He was a shapely thighed kid and a fine pioneer, the likes of which you don't see anymore nowadays, but forever brooding about something. And I was ecstatic when, as we were leaving at summer's end, he handed his Moscow address and phone number to me as a gesture toward a continuing friendship. The bugler was sounding taps and a bunch of people were getting a bonfire going on the soccer field, clamoring and roaring, pinching girls slightly older than themselves in immodest places, while Vadim and I stood beyond the brouhaha beneath the lonesome stars cloaked in nocturnal beauty, joyously clasping hands. Then, suddenly, while making our adieus, he goes and confides to me the ailing anguish that has been gnawing at him, because of which he was evidently drawn to me unconsciously, as if to a fellow victim. Last winter, while playing air guns at home, he had accidentally shot and killed his little four-year-old sister. "But it was just an accident, right? An accident!" I muttered, completely dumbfounded, not knowing how to deal with the sudden sinking feeling in my heart and knowing instinctively that all was lost, that there could no longer ever be a friendship between us. And he was already bolting off, wailing, dispersing among the bushes into the polka dots of his sunny yellow sports shirt after jerking his hand from my clammy, white, bloodless fingers—our grip loosened. "I'll give you a buzz as soon as I get home, Vadim!" I solemnly promised into thin air, keenly aware at that moment that there would never be a time or a reason I would call.

Of course, by that time, mind you, I myself had two victims hanging over my head, Nikolai and Pavel. But just the same, despite my generous nature and my own ostracism, I could not set foot across the line that separated me from that only child, Vadim, who had bunglingly shot his baby sister to death. I had betrayed him, cravenly, despicably. What, then, can I ask of others?

In my archive there is a pile of these episodes, inexplicable and inextricable—go ahead and organize a protest demonstration at the Last Judgment. Sometime I'll describe all this in more detail. But, for now, I shall divulge publicly two pieces of information that have not, up to now, had any direct bearing on me.

The first episode takes place in the country. A child about five years old (of which there are many) chucks a rock at a neighbor's rooster that strayed too far into his garden, knocking it stone dead in the head. The old lady, owner of the rooster, not meaning anything more than to throw a scare into the little scamp, pushes him into the pigpen with her sow. His father comes home. The old lady tells him her story. They unbolt the pen—ostensibly to punish the rascal, but the porker is already chomping on the last few morsels. The father runs to go get an axe, and bashes the old lady's brains in.

Another little boy, in the city, was sent by his mother to the store with ten rubles. The family was poor and ten rubles was a lot of money to them. He reports back without a kopeck to his name. He lost 'em. She was ironing the linen and in a fit of blind rage hurled a brush at him. He whimpers, throws a tantrum, goes tramping off to bed, and hides behind the door. She goes on with the ironing. The father comes home. Where's Vovka? Why, he's been a real pain-in-the-you-know-what. . . . They go to look—Vovka's dead. Hit in the temple. The father says that he'll go to the police station since a report has to be filed. He comes home with the police to find her— swinging from the end of a rope.

I draw blanks when I hear such stories, and I can't come up with an explanation. In every case, in absolutely every case, the culprit is triviality, stupidity, some natural error, the invisible jinx. A brush. A rock. A vicious circle. But at least in those cases there were dark forces controlling the heart's movements. Whereas in my case, there is only good behind it all. I'm ashamed to admit it, but I only want what's best for people. I'll bend over backward, but everything gets all twisted the other way around.

I realize that what I am writing and saying is insane. But some kind of abnormality has crept into reality. A kind of dislocation. You live in complete paranoia. I think I should be sitting quietly like a patient on my mental hospital bed, convulsed in silent laughter. . . .

There is, after all, such a thing as coincidence! I want to help a blind old man cross the street. I take him under the arm, exercising extreme care, and he goes and falls down, as if on purpose, breaking his cane or shattering his glasses, and is the first to turn around and press charges. Why get involved? Wouldn't it be better to skulk around a blind man before it's too late? No sooner have you offered money to a beggar-woman than immediately your goodness makes the bored corner cop's cup of forbearance run over. Off he carts the tramp for immobilizing currency from circulation in accordance with the governmental directive for combating mendicancy and social parasitism.

In the depths of despair, just to see what might happen, I would try doing nasty things. I vaguely recall once, as I was walking along, kicking a drunkard sprawled out on the sidewalk. And you know what? Everything turned out all right; nothing came of it. He got up, reeling, and zipped off, making a beeline straight for home, as if that were the only normal thing to do. With no muttering or cursing. Then one member of the crowd commends and sanctions my brave deed. "It's about time. They shouldn't be scumming up the capital in front of diplomats and all. And anyway, comrade, you've saved that vagabond from a sure mugging while sleeping on a public thoroughfare. And maybe from nephritis. . . ."

Little did all these surmises comfort me. 'Cause you still don't know where the guy you got off his duff with a kick in the pants is off to and how he'll end up. But even evil in its pure form doesn't interest us, doesn't make us happy. Evil is merely a by-product of the good we tarry for. . . .

Out of all this hullabaloo, I took up smoking. And I smoked so much that my lung X rays began to look, for all intents and purposes, like my black coat. On the other hand, in the spirit of family tradition, I decided to get a dog. I thought I'd just take in and give a home to some stray that had wandered into our garbage bin. There have been precedents, you know! I hoped that it might brighten my memories.

The dog is, in my opinion, closer to man than other animals. By sole virtue of the fact that dogs have a sense of humor—neither cats nor horses are capable of that. The dog alone, if you think about it, whisks its tail about just like a fan. It laughs, albeit through tears. You watch a dog lying on its side on the floor: suddenly its tail starts wagging! That means it's imagining and dreaming something. That means it's a scrivener, a writer, a dog, just like the rest of us, like you and me. It whimpers in its sleep. Sobs. It's tough for everyone, for man and beast alike. When I am with her (not with "it" but "her," since dogs are she-animals) I kind of shake myself off, rise up onto my legs—with these big, separately maneuverable pricked ears. Big and fluttery, like butterfly wings.

And what, may we ask, if she came from my father? Found me all by herself? By scent. Came out of nowhere into the garbage. As an inheritance. She never ages. The Dog of an Enemy of the People is, after all, expected to wait for her master. And I was already having a foretaste of how I, the empty shell of a man over sixty, would whistle for her to come go for a walk late at night, just before bedtime, thinking to myself that for all practical purposes, the day is over—wrapped up—and that all there is left to do is take the dog out and meander along the cool alleyways. She stands motionless, watching, on four paws, as I, on my two feet, can barely drag myself along. Her pupils glint, expectant. She is grateful that I took my overcoat off the hanger and went out with her for a walk. She's just a puppy, yet she understands everything. . . . Wind. Freedom. Drizzling rain. Puddles underfoot. Cobblestones. But we walk and walk. My dog and I. What a landscape. . . .

Or, I imagine it's springtime, and she's about to have puppies. Inexperienced, still too young, she climbs up into my arms in fear, into my neatly made bed. And I myself am apprehensive; I have never delivered puppies before. But she's shaking, huddles close in trustfulness, pleading, and then her puppies come almost crawling out, yes, crawling out of her stomach, one after another. I pet her, coax her: "Don't be afraid. Come on, push a little! It's OK, you're with me. . . ." And they keep pouring out as if from a sack attached to some kind of rope, bedraggled, naked, and only with great difficulty I remember—"umbilical cord," "scissors." I grope about, begin snipping, and she helps me with her teeth, whining, delivers the fifth, or who knows, the sixth and last bundle. And I think, while delivering my dog's puppies, "It's gonna be just like this when we go, bailing out of ourselves, shivering and transfixed with fear." And then the Lord God himself will tuck us cozily into bed when we begin to clamber our way up, saying, "Come on, come on! Don't be afraid, don't be afraid of anything. . . ." And he'll pet us on our bed. . . .

I'm writing about the dog instead of myself. But it's more innocent that way. "Dog," I exclaim, "you are responsible for me from now on! You and you alone!" I, too, was a dog before my brothers. I cowered, kowtowed, lied—nothing availed. . . .

The dog was jabbering. I gave her a cube of sugar. She took it. She munched on it, smacking her lips. I meant to pet her, to pat her ears while contemplating what noble name to give her and suddenly—she turned on me. Not that it hurt very much, but the fact that she bit me in unabashed fury made it twice as hard for me to take. Especially since I am not afraid of dogs, nor do I hate them. It's one thing if I had jerked my hand away or had taken fright, but it didn't happen that way. I held out my hand . . . "You idiot!"

"Fine," I said, bandaging my finger, "I give you sugar and you go and bite me! You go ahead and live in the kitchen. That's too bad for you. You just keep your distance from me from now on!"

She bared her teeth in response. Tiny ones, like those a corpse flashes in the coffin. But, it ran through my mind, what if the damned dog knows something? What if she senses the kind of person she's dealing with? Did she recognize me? Was she taking advantage of me? Don't mess around with good intentions, I tell myself over and over again. Live by yourself, like Mama instructed you. Just as you are approaching someone, suffused with gratitude and with all the best and most shining attributes that still remain within you, then keep in mind what it is you bear. We are separated from death by a glass wall. Ask any hardened murderer if you don't believe me. And the majority of crimes, they'll tell you, are committed not out of malice, not through premeditation, but "just worked out that way in the turn of events." Not that anyone willed it. Not that anyone even tried. The human skull is that thin. The temple is even more fragile. Hit it and you'll see. It'll be as a curse unto you. It'll suddenly dawn on you, "I didn't mean to!" Ha! Didn't mean to? Then why did you come so close, why did you touch the glass which separates us from reality? Abel! Abel! Cain, where is your brother? . . .

Put a barrier before man and he'll cross it. What a fool I was, why the hell did I go off to Volodya's on Mama's birthday without calling first? I was planning on wishing her a happy birthday to redeem my negligence. I could even do that without bothering her precious son. The main thing was to see Mama again. To apologize for talking back, to have a word together after so long. . . .

Volodya occupied the fifth floor of a government residence near a movie theater. He was a minister, if not higher. A maharaja. But I'll bet in his heart he bethought humble and democratic notions of himself, as do all big wheels of his rank. . . . In the plush lobby (naturally, what else?) the doorkeeper on duty, a real Amazon, caught sight of me. She was wearing a semimilitary jacket, without epaulets surprisingly enough, and open-toed shoes, but was in knee-highs as if she were just a regular sort of person.

"Whadda ya want? What address you lookin' for?"

She proceeded to stare me down. . . .

I only came up to her solar plexus, up to the button on her jacket, and that was standing on my toes. But that didn't faze me. When you're happy—and I was feeling a buoyant elation in anticipation of my imminent reunion with Mama and my brother—you get a bit cocky.

"I'm here to see Likhosherst on the fifth floor."

"Affiliation?"

A formal interrogation.

"I'm a relative. See? I'm his brother! My mother works here watching the twins—you know, a nanny. Maybe you've seen them? . . ."

In any case, she had second thoughts about asking me for my identification. If she had, the discrepancy would have been obvious. If I had had to explain why my last name was Sinyavsky . . . I zoomed up the elevator. I buzzed. On the other side of the panel some nice music started playing, like at the entrance to the Hermitage. There palm trees and fondling fronds await you. I notice that there's a large landing for a single renter laid in checkerboard tile on the fifth floor. There is a flower in a flowerpot sitting atop a wrought-iron candlestick. All that's missing is a pool with a peacock. In fact, both the pool and the peacock were most likely hiding inside the palace. Once again, I dauntlessly press the button; it chimes a tune. . . .

Mama came to the door in our familiar old Chinese lion housecoat, but no sooner had I wished her a happy birthday than she started coming toward me across the landing, quietly but not completely shutting the tall oak door behind her. Her expressionless face white as a sheet, she came at me, making either to embrace me or to admonish me about something urgent that she wanted to screen from the others. Terror shone in her eyes as if she had seen a ghost.

"Go away! *Go away*!! Right now, SCRAM!" she hissed, spreading wide the side-folds of her Japanese kimono like a mother hen attacking a hawk to protect her chicks.

"What have you come for? Enough! . . . Haven't you already finished four of them off? That's plenty from you! Don't you come near my fifth! My last! Spare the little ones!!!"

Mama kept advancing toward me as I kept retreating edgewise slowly down the staircase, step by step, hugging the handrail until, under her scorching gaze, I went hurtling down the abyss, half a flight of stairs in a single bound, until I somehow came to an hour later at home.

6

When I appeared the dog gave no sign of moving. They know which side their bread is buttered on. Well, come here, traitor! There's no other name for you. You betrayer! You parasite! You shameful creature, turning cat-in-pan, using your fangs to repel a hand extended in friendship. . . .

No response. There she sits in the dark, in a corner of the kitchen, listening to me and to my every movement, my every breath.

And I? I had really gone out of my way for her. Dogs, I used to exclaim, are more honest than people; they hide nothing behind their backs—they don't have it in them to hide things. They are not here to serve or befriend people, but only as a token of our edification. The dog is the moral standard and positive hero whom I have identified and brought to literature for the only time in my entire, baneful life. Here is a model for you, I would say—the dog. . . .

She didn't even scratch. She sat under the table, silent as an owl, waiting for something. Somehow she just didn't trust me. Or had she caught the smell of death that always followed on my heels? Could she read my soul? Could she see the future? . . .

"Come off it! Don't exaggerate the dog's power!" I said to

reassure myself. "Don't follow that one's footsteps. You know it only leads to a bad end. . . ."

At this point, groping along without turning on the light, I opened the back door that led to the yard and the garbage bin. It was where she had once appeared to flirt with me. She had come of her own accord; no one had called her. I let out a roar in a voice not my own: "Get out of here, you villain! The way is clear! Find yourself another haven. Get as far away from sin as you can, before it's too late. Get out of harm's way, dog. . . ."

No, I did not throw her out. I set the base creature free: let her live. . . .

From out back came the smell of fresh air, of cold, of autumn, of melting snow. I never did get to take her for a walk, not even once. . . . In the darkness it was impossible to make out whether she had disappeared or not. Most likely she had disappeared, evaporated without a sound or a trace, like a thief in the night. With her tail between her legs, and without a look back, she went out into the night, into the rain, back to where she'd come from—to the devil even, just to get as far away from me as possible. . . .

With a sort of nonchalant gesture I kicked off my boots and only afterward took off my overcoat. Trying to knock some sensation into my skull I gave it a shake, hard enough to make my teeth chatter. Creeping sideways into the bathroom, I carefully aimed in the familiar direction and took a leak. Then I drank some water. I could remember and identify by feel every little convolution in our building. My feet were soaked and my forehead and cheeks burning, and at first it was hard to tell whether I was hot or cold. The sweat seemed to be coming to a boil at the roots of my hair. And then, with no advance warning, a chill suddenly came over me. . . .

If the dog hadn't run off, she would have been cuddling up to me now, yawning, poking her slobbery face with her wet nose into my outstretched hand, and I would have lain down, tripe-like, beside her without any discussion. My bones were pleading for it. My back was moaning to lie down right there beside the dog on the kitchen floor, and without delay. Just to press my forehead to its plastic surface: you too, maternal-material, are inseparable from your son, even if you are synthetic! . . . And that same dog will lay her head on your smooth foot. . . .

It is nice to lie on the floor and think about nothing. Or you can arrange your elbow in a comfortable position, with your chin settled just under the crook of your arm and your extremities all spread out freely, and lean on that elbow, and just feel like a King. And once again the night will be filled with paper and flame. White pages tinged with black and scattered all over the floor and up to the ceiling. . . .

Bells sounded in my ears. That was the refrigerator humming, the gift from Ol' Volodya. It worked as if it were paid to. Nobody asked it to, nobody was supervising, but just the same it worked its heart out, with the precision of a Red Navy sailor. Suddenly I was touched with pity and respect for that refrigerator. If you want a good example to follow, take the refrigerator. It won't let you down, it won't deceive you. . . .

I never did turn on the lights, though, because of the cockroaches. Since Mama left they had been breeding by the stove. . . . O my Lord! How much life there is bubbling all around us. Life—invisible, inoffensive life—dog-life and cockroach-life. And it is all the more amazing because it doesn't depend on us, somehow it is separate from us even though we are all interconnected. What would they ever do without us? Of course, we do execute them periodically, but we still uphold the very fact of the cockroach's existence, against our will. We feed it and keep it warm. If you come out at night to put on the water for tea, their front ranks will be out in formation, armor and helmets shining. What are they gathering for? A rally? A debate? And then they retreat without a sound into the corners when a light comes on. As soon as you set foot in the kitchen it's as if they had never existed. . . .

Or do cockroaches feel the writer's intent gaze fixed on them—about to brush them off the wall and squash them in one instinctive motion? Just at the thought of it they jump up and run off! But then, it was mutual fear and double apprehension. Is the cockroach's brain so finely organized that it finds a single stray thought so repellent and base that it is tantamount to murder? Or, on the other hand, is it that they see a bit farther down the path of history and read people's hearts like a book, and so hold power over us? . . .

That is why I did not turn on the lights but groped my way in the dark on this occasion: it was safer that way. Have no fear, cockroaches, I'm not here! It really is comforting to remember that in a hundred years—two hundred at the most—you will no longer exist. The grass will grow over everything. You'll be forgotten. Effaced from memory. Shrouded in mist. Just try whistling for your Little Jinx then, Mama! . . .

During this reverie I burned a hole in my pants with my

cigarette in the dark. They were the only pants I had. The only ones for my whole life. That's what happens: in two hours only five minutes had passed, maybe even less. Time is short. You won't get a chance to pray. You can't even form your hand into an uncertain three-fingered sign anymore, to cross yourself. . . .

Quietly I undressed and lay down. Actually, I didn't lie down, but jumped into bed in my underwear, the way people jump into cold water. That was the only way—just get it over with. What is more, whenever I lie down gently I am struck from above with a coughing fit. This time I avoided that. I hid under the covers and warmed up. I closed my eyes as if I were asleep. That helped me get a step up. But even here the apparition caught up with me from the landing on the stairway. Mama was advancing upon me, spreading her wings and senselessly whispering: "Get out! Spare him! Leave the fifth alone! Spare the puppies!"

As if she were hiding behind her back, behind that strong oak door, not an omnipotent magnate, but a little boy like me. . . . She advanced and I retreated from step to step, until I could stand her scorching gaze no longer and hurtled down the stairs, coming to under the warmth of my own blanket.

Oh, sleep at last! I was quaking. . . .

In my dream the dog was scratching and scraping at the back door to come back in. "Is that you, Dora?" I asked in my dream. "I'm getting up right now." It kept scratching. "Is that you, Mama?" I asked again, although I realized that it was neither Dora nor Mama scratching but the dog I had thrown out, asking to come in again through the back door. "I'll open up right away!" But for some reason I didn't get up, I just kept hoping and longing for her return and trying to pull myself together: look, it's only nerves! How long can a person tremble like this, inexpressibly? I'd have gone to sleep with pleasure, except that my legs kept cramping. . . .

By the way, I know no other definition of prose—not to mention verse—than a trembling of some sort of little bell in the sky. You know how it is, sometimes it's all over, but the bell keeps vibrating; it is inexplicable, but the sound still reaches your ears from far away, from the other end of the world. . . . Ever since then, whenever I am sent a story or a poem to review, I read it and ask myself, before giving my assessment, *could you hear the bell? Was a string vibrating in the blue yonder? Or was this just a product of the mind, of idleness, of emotion? . . . It never fails. . . .*

"Devil! devil! devil! devil!" She screamed right at me, advancing on me and screwing up her face to frighten me. She must have noticed something in me that was dark and foreign to what I was and what I really am. I was puzzled; Mama was cutting me to the quick. I threw myself again and again at her feet and prayed for her to look at me once more, more carefully. Did I really resemble what she took me for? And at the same time, by some strange prompting I found myself transfixed, sharing her bitter right to hurl insults in my face.

"Devil! devil! devil!" She kept screaming with jealousy and rage, driving me back with each new word into the blackness whence I had come and which I fled and feared, for I recognized this trait in myself, this ill-fate whereby my very presence vexed and tormented people. "Get out, get out! This very second! . . ."

The Lord saved me: I woke up.

Only toward morning was I visited by an image that had some semblance of reality, one that promised salvation, perhaps, from the nocturnal dance of terror. I dozed a bit and saw what looked like a pleasant woodland glade through which strolled either a slender girl or, oddly enough, a pure-bred dog of rare beauty. Wearing a shaggy dress and collar and led on a chain, she ambled ahead of a fabulous peasant in a fur coat, whose broad, bearded face made you instantly recall that there still were evil people on earth who would tyrannize over a creature of such unique nobility and grace. He shouted rudely at her, tugged her by the chain, and brandished his whip at her for some unknown offense she had committed against him, and she began rushing about and suddenly tore from her leash and dashed up a tree, the way ermines do as they flee from the hunter's pursuit. But what was even harder to comprehend was that, ascending the branches like a staircase, she threw off the dress that the wind had been twisting around her and, flashing her desperate, sunlit nakedness, suddenly reached the top. From there she flew off, flapping her wings like a bird. All this took only a few moments, and the bird, slipping off into the sky, formed the natural continuation of the whirlwind the fugitive had created in twisting out of the clothes as they flew from her body, and she also fulfilled the promise of the tree, which was very tall and pointed and seemed predestined to serve as a runway. With a curse, the peasant set off after the girl, climbing easily up the trunk. As he climbed he, too, threw off his confining caftan, but he was less self-assured and clumsier in his movements and he got stuck halfway up, just as the bird took off from the branch. . . .

How happy I was for her! Next morning I had the thought that we too, God willing, would gain freedom from our slavery, from the chains of the unwilled evil we set in motion—myself, and Mama, and Volodya, and the dog. . . . What is the point of these personal vendettas, this search for the culprit? Everyone deserves to be rejected. And everyone deserves to be embraced. . . . How little we need. It really can happen that you dream of something radiant— even if you don't know what it is—and it makes you feel better than a king, you sing and make prognoses, and you think, "I will fly away! I will fly away! And my troubles will be over!"

But alas, the dream did not come true, at least not at this juncture in the story. And Mama, no matter how hard she tried to drive me from the doors, still could not protect her offspring from my black advent. A month later the Likhoshersts' former personal chauffeur came to see me, for old time's sake and to get the stuff Mama had left behind. From the chauffeur all the details of what had happened came to light.

Mama had scarcely ushered me off the landing and returned to the table in Volodya's abode when he started in with questions: who was at the door, and what for, and how come. She tried in vain to weave a lie—"It seems they had the wrong floor." Suspecting something was wrong, he phoned the doorkeeper on the first floor.

"What? Little Jinx? And you didn't let him in? You chased him off? My brother? Your own son? Kept him from my birthday cake? Then I'll invite him! I demand it! Bring him here!"

In a word, it was Sodom and Gomorrah in the house. Mama herself was sorry about her deception at that moment.

He, this powerful public figure, rushed off without his coat or hat to bring me back. I don't know why—perhaps it was the whim of a petty tyrant, or the voice of blood-ties, or a feeling of some awakening guilt toward me—or perhaps he was trying to prove to someone that, despite his lofty position and status, he was still a regular guy, simple and considerate, like everyone in his field. In any case, forgetting his prejudices, Vladimir trumpeted through the whole entryway: "Little Jinx! Where have you gone? Please come join us! . . ."

I had vanished without a trace. But even without setting foot over his threshold or laying eyes on him, I still delivered the death sentence to my brother from afar. He cut across the vestibule like a bull, leapt out the door, and started running back and forth. Apparently something went off in his head and he dashed past the streetlights after someone, running against the traffic. At this point, a dump truck speeding around the traffic circle ran right into him. . . .

"The fellow's on trial now," added the chauffeur in a melancholy voice as he packed up the belongings.

"What fellow?" I asked in bewilderment.

"The truck driver, of course. Killing a public figure like that, as if he were a simple working guy! They could even blow it up into a political scandal if they wanted to. But, be honest, as a citizen—however upset you may be about your brother—you've got to admit: was it the driver's fault? How could he stop at such a speed? And do you think his was the only dump truck there? The ones behind would have crashed into him. The light was green! . . ."

After that Mama and I never saw each other again. And a year later, when she quietly passed away, I didn't join the funeral procession. To be honest, I was afraid of coming into contact with her grandchildren, with the wife. I didn't have the strength of character to face them. And besides, I wanted them to remain among the living. . . . Those puppies were my nieces and nephews, after a fashion.

7

Once I was walking down New Arbat Boulevard and I saw Dora. Not the second Dora, the one I had fallen for out of stupidity and the tenderness of my years, but the other one, the Good Fairy, Dora Aleksandrovna. This time she appeared in the distance in the grocery department of a huge, Moscow-wide supermarket and was weighing out candy for someone with her little porcelain hand, and flour for someone else. She hadn't changed a bit. For me, she had even grown younger compared to my early memories of her; or perhaps I had by that time already truly aged myself. But an inner voice told me that this was she, Dora Aleksandrovna herself, in the past a pediatric doctor and now an exuberant and elegant retail saleswoman.

At first I studied her from the boulevard at a distance, through the thick-glassed store window, becoming more and more convinced of my discovery's plausibility with each successive nonpareil gesture. And then, having worked up my nerve, I walked in inconspicuously. What a bonanza! Golden tangerines. Sprats. Bulk sausage. Hunter's links. Wines from every country and of every sort in a variety of bottles in a section finished in oak veneer especially to complement that form of packaging, right across, incidentally, from the cherished department in which my lovely temptress was whirling on stage, above her soap and salt. . . .

I do not know, gentlemen, whether you have ever had the good fortune smile on you of seeing such mountains of comestibles and spirits during a free moment of the day when there aren't yet so many people around as to spoil a leisurely and thorough browse through the sundry items. But even if you see this panorama every single day, you will not understand or appreciate what I'm talking about, and you may fancy the fantastic riches laid out behind glass display cases and parading along the walls high to the sky in the shape of columns, mausoleums, eastern grottoes, porticos, castles, Carthages—all built with slabs of creamery butter, jars of jam, vanilla rusk, piecrust, cinnamon, eggs, and other spices—to be something banal, run-of-the-mill, perhaps even mediocre in comparison to what you have at times gotten to see abroad or partook of before the Revolution. Of course, it's another matter if you come from a village or provincial town which barely gets the radio and newspapers from the capital and from which the large buffets crammed chock-full to overflowing with foodstuffs (you could shop a hundred years and still not buy everything) attract waves of dreamy-eyed provincials. In that case, you'll have eyes, a tongue, and hands with which to express it more appropriately and vividly, so you can see and feel, stuffing sacks, jam-packing your bags, shouting yourself hoarse, screaming bloody murder for another kilogram of ham, exchanging again and again the bills you have sewn into your underwear, ensconced in the lining of your coat and in your bras—all to the delight of the pudge-faced Moscow winos and to the joy of swift pickpockets.

But imagine, for a man of a different stripe, who has neither a father nor a mother, no city or town to his name, it's as if he had never even tasted any of these delicacies but had only read about them in old-fashioned novels. An ordinary roll would satisfy his hunger, the kind that in the good old days were called "French rolls" but are known nowadays as "city rolls." But he doesn't even remember that. He wanders from counter to counter, satiated, it seems, by sole virtue of the toxic odors of the cheeses, the nauseating stench of the meat and fish stall, the rich aroma of ground coffee thick enough to make you faint, the light, slightly acrid powder of the parceled sugar. So, you say that sugar has no smell? Well then, just take a whiff, get a whiff of that! . . .

But don't imagine for a second that I, carried away by the sumptuous food, had lost sight of the goal of my visit, Dora. No, she was indeed the queen of the ball and the genius loci of the premises, which served for her as a marvelous backdrop. Out of the corner of my eye, I did not tire of following her light-blue apron and lace headdress, which fluttered over the stage like a moth. There was no line at her grocery counter, and after enough pussyfooting around, I decided to get a little closer. Although, at first, without raising my eyes out of a sense of propriety, I peered through the teas which had been set on display in the lower compartment in cheerful little wrappers. "Georgian Extra," "Krasnodar Type II," "Chinese," "Indian," and even "Ceylon." Not half bad!

No shoving and grabbing. The tea-boxes sat there like little schoolgirls at a final exam, well-dressed, rosy-cheeked, and waiting for nothing more than what grade they would get in algebra or geography. . . . Aromatic tea, medicinal tea, the forbidden tea, Vitamin C-fortified tea, antitubercular tea, gum-astringent tea, tea that envelops your soul with red, hot, oily fat that gets your heart working nonstop like a clock, tea whose strength has been set to rival rum's and is apportioned by the grain, to the very thickest with the consistency of jelly that is best of all taken—I'll let you in on the secret—with a little piece of salted herring. Tea on a par with the felt boots, quilted pants, riding boots, and sweaters that get dropped off at the prison camp with the same kind of nonchalance with which the sage Adenauer exchanged his equipment for five packages of tea, tea that slaps together the funds, that carves out a career, and that even cost some their heads, was being made available to individuals in unlimited quantities at a fabulously low price. . . .

"What do you need, Pops?" rang out the melodious voice that sometime long ago had asked me: "What do you want, little fella? What are you crying for?" I wrested my attention away from the delightful packages of tea, which had been playing the part of an overture to this soprano voice, and my eyes locked with those of the grocery woman, soaring above me like a bird that had flown away in a dream and had now descended to earth in the form of a miraculous blonde. She appeared to be about seventeen, not a year older. And to stare at her, at those eternally blossoming features giving off resplendent rays, was as unbearable as looking at the sun, even if we reach out to it, dream, and burn with its lights. That's how it is, I recall, during adolescence, when you're afraid of offending with a glance or confession the girl who has caught your fancy, and each step you take or word you utter in her direction seems indiscreet, risqué, so that you end up losing her to some persistent, well-built double-crosser. Even though I had, since then, after years of experience, made headway through the hard knocks of life, although I had become wiser and stauncher, although I had developed, I was expecting the ground to open once again and swallow me up in the presence of this girl who had plucked me from the air simply with her innocent look and the regal tension of her questioning face. Did she realize what was happening to me, that I was shrinking up into a little ball, that I was dissolving, depreciating, turning into that sick, helpless child that lay before her some forty odd years ago, stark naked in my squeaky little crib? Ah, she was pretending that she didn't understand, that she didn't recognize me, and fluttered about the tea-plantation, turning here and there in various directions with her little ceramic hand that was like the neck of a teapot in curved readiness to pour you an exquisite drink. . . . And not even a hint of the stammer of our first and last meeting.

"What do you want, Pops?" she repeated musically, tracing her nacre little finger along the whole garden, the sugar, the tea with the extravagant tags, the pepper, and the vermicelli.

Her gesture was imbued, if you will, with the grace of Venus de' Medici, or someone else of that ilk.

"Well, Hon', I'm lookin' to see what tea I might be takin'," I replied, whispering like some old fogey, like some hick from inner Chukhlom.

"I recommend the Ceylon tea, Pops!"

"Thanks, you're a dear. We think that Ceylon will suit us just fine. Say, you don't just happen to be from Ceylon yourself? Or from somewhere even farther out?"

And plucking up my mettle, I looked up. I just stood and stared piercingly. Could it possibly *not* be her? It *was* her. It *was!* In her gigantic eyes splashed two, no, all in all three, goldfish. . . . You will probably be surprised: why three and not two? Oh, naive people! Why, because she, Dora, had such eyes, such eyes that from time to time they would splash out onto her entire face and play there, like three goldfish. . . .

"Well, Little Jinx," she said, her smile fading on her lips, "got any other tall tales for us? Do you need something, old man? You out now? For good?"

"Yeah, for good," I said. "Straight from the train station. No roof to cover my head. But, Dora Aleksandrovna, I do need one thing from you: who was my father? And whence my heinous crime, for which I keep paying the price, or at least part of it? Why, I ask you, when I only want what's best, why do I bring everyone misery? And may I not tag on to the afresh-mentioned question a request? To give me back my old stammer, if that's what it takes, my old childhood dumbness and feebleness, just so I can live and let live, like all normal people, not causing anybody any particular problems? . . ."

"Goodness!" exclaimed Dora. "So many questions! My, haven't we been keeping a regular 'complaints and suggestions box' locked up in our cash register! Whereas before, you were a little boy more on the shy side. But with age . . . hold on a second," she said. "First let me serve this customer. See? They're ganging up like dogs that haven't been fed in three days! What'll it be, Miss, half a kilo of macaroni. . . ?"

And she began darting about once again, like lightning, back and forth along the counter. I stepped back to admire how expertly she handled her solo role. It was simply some kind of Spanish dance of a saleswoman serving an impatient public. Everyone is pushing checks, baskets, and oil-flasks toward her. "Just a minute, Comrade! Not everybody all at once!" she snaps. But the more carefully I traced her aerial dance steps, which were simultaneously connected to the gold mine in the air of scarce grocery items, the clearer it became that while dancing and haggling Dora had not stopped talking to me in her own way, not unlike the heavenly host, by means of winks and nods, periphrastic allegories and symbols whose precise signification left nothing to the imagination. One moment she's presenting somebody with some salt from the flat of her hand with a barely perceptible smile, in the next, she's upraising a vessel over her head, she's proffering olive oil to the spectators. And then, no sooner has she performed an entrechat than the requested cigarettes find themselves already clasped in her fingers, a deluxe brand with the mysterious transcription: "Herzegovina Flor"! You have got to understand this! . . .

But, strangely enough, I got the impression that the brawling throng of shoppers did not put up the slightest fuss as the enchantress, all but ignoring customer preference, meted out her potions, of her own accord, and chosen in harmony with a sign language meant not for them, but for me. And each of them gratefully carted off what he had received, holding it close to his heart. Or maybe she was controlling them with body language or had cast a spell over the crowd? Or maybe they, like petty Soviet menials, were working as her backups, as extras conspiring with this fairy-witch in her language of pantomime, through which she was attempting to communicate with me, her poor client? . . .

At any rate, I watch: it's like a picture show! And then the strangest thing happened! She fills up an old woman's entire handbag with yeast and gestures to her with her chin, "Get out of here, I'm tellin' ya, Granny, before you get ripped off!" But this, gentlemen, was actually an ultimatum put to me or, so to speak, a "historical alternative," and by accepting it, I dared to hope for something, in that Dora might answer my question. Just think it through: Yeast! Yeast! Like the premise in a logic problem. Yeast, as everyone knows, as far back as in ancient Greece, presupposed meat-filled pies, a roaring feast, a wedding, drunkenness, a still in your own house . . . and there was something in the way she wrapped the yeast in a paper cone that was menacing and at the same time joyously called out to me to come under her white arm. It was as if Dora had said, "Watch out! I'll make you happy! Marry me and you'll see! And let's perform the wedding this very night! Make up your mind! . . ."

My jaw dropped in astonishment; I could not believe my eyes. Is this, I think to myself, what you would have me understand? Does this not purport to be some sort of fleeting allusion to marriage? Isn't marrying me just in your scheme of mocking fate and free will, if you'll pardon the expression? Me? ME? And she replies "yes" with a dance step as a sign of consent so that I could get a surer sense of it. And then, in frustration, she strews some spices into an envelope for the caller next in line. As if to say, "I know you'll deliberate long and hard, you'll try to weigh both sides, but remember, I can make you one mean well-spiced pie!" And come on, if a woman offers to make you happy, it would be a crying shame to be suspicious of her offer; in fact, there's a risk in mistrusting it. . . . Well, Little Jinx, I say to myself, looks like it's a race against time—and time is running out.

Not that I had anything against getting married, but it's just that I hadn't given it a thought in a long while. Ever since childhood, girls had shunned me like the plague. But I could rest easy on Dora's account. What a lady! What particular harm would I be capable of doing her? Why, she could certainly run circles around any old devil. Of course, I was kind of old for her. And my face didn't go right with hers. Nor did my posture. I'd grown shabby. And I didn't have the necessary prospects for family life now: no steady salary, no housing, not even a housing permit . . . the question is, where the hell would we have a wedding and why the hell go through with it anyway? . . .

And just imagine, at that very moment she waves anew her magic little hand in every direction like a genuine ballerina, as if she were shooing off flies, and motions to the auditorium packed with countless treasures. Heh, heh, I get it, why, she rules the roost, with the whole police force, the city council, and the prosecutor's office in her pecking order. Sugar, cereal, flour, more than one could ever possibly know what to do with. . . . And I had good reason for suddenly feeling down in the mouth; where in the world were we supposed to get our guests for the wedding feast from? After all, I didn't know a living soul in Moscow, as Dora Aleksandrovna laid out five bars of soap for someone onto a newspaper. Now take note, Sinyavsky, is that soap or something more? But for the life of me I never figured out what that soap meant.

I did begin to cheer up, however, as befits a fiancé, and even started to perform a one-legged jig. Jolly good show! See, if I marry Dora, my house and kitchen will be like clockwork. In the morning, I'll say, "Dora, dear, please make me a pork chop for breakfast. No, order a marinated miller's thumb. No, better yet, whip me up two fried eggs and toast—" or toward evening she'll come flying home from the store on the wings of love with her shopping bag full of groceries, and all my bitter thoughts, sorrows, and ills will flutter away like moths.

As I was looking on, the whole store somehow came alive. The chandelier was lighted. The crowd thickened. I wouldn't exactly say they were dancing, but something rhythmical, intense, fell across their faces. They rubbed shoulders, their heels tapped, they communicated by winks. Someone began singing softly to the accompaniment of an accordion, "If only I had gilded mountains, rivers filled with wine. . . ." Had my goddess once and for all entranced them with her hypnotic nuptial passes? Or was I just light-headed from hunger? From happiness? From the blissful realization that the curse that I had borne so long, like some kind of yoke, would be lifted, yes lifted!

Indeed, I thought, in song and dance everyone is purified by getting away from himself, leaving the body, the decay, to go to a higher plane, as they did in ancient times. The cathartic meaning of rhythm was known to Dora, who, while distributing her highly marketable goods around Moscow, did not disregard poetry, and in perfect accord with it broke the spell and the terror with fluid motions. The spell—of death, terror—in the face of life, before the original sin of my own unbearable face. . . . People, my brethren, I say to myself, arms outspread, what if on all the continents, in order to be paid or offered a kopeck, we stand like Christs, all on the same level, blocking passage. And maybe the wedding ceremony is taking place right this very minute. Maybe we're not standing in a store, but actually in a church. A church in an ancient cathedral where, with her hands, the fairy is curing and crowning king her pauperized prospect. . . .

In short, I became so brazen and sure of myself in my own eyes that, abandoning my observation post, I cut right up to the grocery counter without standing in line.

"Miss!" I addressed her. "I urge you not to forget to throw in some bay leaves, just for me. The parishioners need some for the holiday. . . ."

"Well, look at you now, asking for bay leaves!" she shook her finger at me. "Sir, we've been out of bay leaves for ages. Are you sure you won't have some pepper, or caraway seeds? . . ."

And three little goldfish flashed, then swam away. Dora Aleksandrovna peered at me meaningfully and smiled somewhat wistfully. . . .

. . . But let us go back to the future. Well, rolling off down the rabbit hole, down a regular rabbit hole. . . . We arrive at her place, at my wife's, that is, driving right on up to her tumbledown shack. Not too bad; livable: a one-bedroom apartment with a built-in bathroom facility. Everything is simple and even modest. No luxury. None of those cheval glasses, bagatelles, or pincushions. Real masculine. Except that there is a little cabinet standing there, I see. The minute I laid eyes on it, I fell in love with it on the spot. An extraordinary little cabinet! It's been with me now to this very day, even though since then I have gone through twenty moves and a lot of things have happened in my life. But that little cabinet is still with me.

For starters and for clarity's sake, let me describe it in words so that it takes on an existence. Imagine: a walnut cabinet on four legs. But how cleverly it's all been designed and put together! Pressed flush against the wall with a tall and slender back, where glass-covered books glittered in gilded bindings. And lower down, below the waist, jutting out half a meter, there is a slanting desk with a cover, with two horizontal slots beneath the walnut. For papers, or if you like, manuscripts, one for rough drafts, one for final drafts. The belly of this little cabinet is unusually handy. And even lower down—and this is the most important thing about it—are its twisted little legs, rather long and unusual for a cabinet, but for that very reason rather stubby, taken with the whole torso. On the whole, then, it looked like a gopher on the steppe, squatting on its hind legs and perking up its front paws to get a better look at everything going on up front beyond the expanse of the steppe sands. Except in this simile, the gopher should not have four legs but six in all, because this little cabinet had squatted down and raised itself up on its four extremities, but its two upper ones seemed to be missing. . . .

"So, Dorochka, you know," I say, "this, my silver fairy, this could well be Ernst Theodor Amadeus Hoffmann his very self on four little feet, dropping by as a special treat! Pay particular attention to the 'Amadeus'! Now tell me the truth: do you understand—do you have any idea—what this little cabinet means in my life? . . ."

"I do," she replies. "Very well, then. It's my dowry to you, Little Jinx. But don't you even so much as think of selling it. . . . Why don't you stop gaping at that cabinet and take a look around? . . ."

I look behind me. Nothing out of the ordinary. A one-room apartment with a built-in bathroom. Oh, yes, it occurs to me that most likely Dora Aleksandrovna had herself in mind with that "take a look around." Every woman is created to be appreciated. Of course she means herself. I encircle her waist with my arms and go for a kiss. She's my wife when it comes right down to it, isn't she? I prod, "Dora," and grope for a button, just as the little punks taught me back in grade school. What can you do? Pleasant dalliance on my part, naturally. . . .

"What are you doing? Are you off your rocker?" She breaks free and pushes my arm away as if it were a toy or something. "All hands, no heart? Don't take that literally. Don't paw me! . . ."

And with these words she puts me in my place. But she's just a saleswoman. She's just a nobody! Who have I gotten myself mixed up with? The same old story, it seems. They say that women play hard to get just to have guys beg. Like performers, "Oh, I couldn't, really; I'm not in voice today! . . ."

I pretend to be discouraged. But in my mind an interesting story line is simultaneously developing. So what? It's better this way. I don't need that. I just don't have to put up with it. Just who does she think she is, Lili Brik or something? So back to the cabinet. At least it will understand me. Hoffmannesque legs. Their cover: a drooping little desk in a carved binding. Books that I have never opened. And in the very fact that I have never opened them lies its charm. I still see it all before me as if it were yesterday. Twisted wood. And its walnut stare. Standing as if rooted to the spot and staring. An idol! What else would you call it? My own private idol!

And in the background I hear that the teapot is already intoning its vesper song. Its spout toots. Books in the cabinet with gilded spines and a teapot in the kitchen. What else could one ask for?

I have barely walked through the daydream, I have barely finished the thought, when Dora's already by my side. Like she's pounding on a keyboard. "All right," she says, "you can't make a leopard change his stripes. Be honest with me, Little Jinx: who do you love more, me or the teapot? Me or the books? Just be honest. . . ."

In my mind, I fall to my knees before her. I kiss the hem of her skirt (again, only mentally).

"But you, of course, Dora Aleksandrovna. That's like comparing apples and oranges! It's you, you, and no one else. And the books—phooey! To hell with them. I can do without 'em! There were times in history when no one read or wrote books. Why should we? And in the second place. . . ."

What was in the first place? I had already forgotten.

"And in the second place, you probably have *Robinson Crusoe* stashed away somewhere in there (I point with my finger). *Treasure Island*. And here (I point again) is *A Thousand and One Nights*. But how can anyone write and read all this? There's not enough time. You know, there was a time when you could spend your whole life poring over one book, leafing through the pages. But if I don't compose something each day I get so ill, Dora. I experience the lack physically, this gaping hole in history. But if I write a sentence, then every-

thing suddenly fits snugly, everything feels calm and so easy—
so easy. . . ."

She listened to me with her hand propped against her
cheek, frowning like a little old Russian lady. She sighed. Not
for herself, but for my sake. How could she be of help to me?
She had provided me with lodging and the comforts of home.
She'd bestowed on me a permanent furniture loan. And in the
kitchen the teapot kept squealing. The cabinet stood motionless, its glass panels shimmering. Let's pull on a robe for life's
warmth and begin reading. . . .

"You're a chip off the old block," she says. "He also traded
his life for paper, to no avail. Drove your mother to the brink,
to the point of having you. . . ."

"My father?" I started, "Where? Who? You promised! . . ."

She gave me a poke in the side with her elbow. Bee! A real
bee. The kind that heals with its sting. It meant, "Don't just
stand there gawking, use your eyes. No, not there, over
here. . . . Warm, cold, cold, getting warmer, warmer. . . .
You're burning up!" The cabinet behind me sat up on its hind
legs and looked on in disbelief. I stared, too.

In the middle of the room is a long banquet table set for
five, no, counting on my fingers, seven. Empty chairs. With
vodka and every kind of hors d'oeuvre imaginable in the
center. Flowers. Something red in a decanter. Forks. Plates.
Something with a meaty aroma tickles my nostrils. . . .

"Sit down and have a bite to eat after your trip. I expect you
haven't eaten in two days. . . . Well, to the good old days!"

And she pours the wine into a wineglass as translucent as
water. You know, such light-tinted ancient wines do exist in
this world. You drink one glass, then another, and your head's

still clear. Take a third, a fourth. Makes no difference. Your head feels as clear as day. A fifth, a sixth, and you're jumping onto your steed with a "Hi-ho, Silver, away!" A fine wine!

But there's no place for us to gallop off *to*. And no other guests are coming. Besides Dora's and my two guest-chairs-of-honor, five were left unoccupied. It's oppressive to eat and drink in the presence of empty chairs. . . .

"Why don't you take a better look?" she goads me. And she just stands there and stares herself. As if she were truly seeing something before her or conjuring images from out of thin air. For real now, out of focus at first and then getting a bit clearer, shapes and indistinct faces started to form around the table. But the contours disappeared, drowned away, and dimmed from sight, requiring some effort to fix them visually.

"I ask you please, however, not to make a commotion if you recognize anyone," she admonished me, "and not to go jumping up out of your seat trying to go after them. It won't do any good—they can't see or hear you. Look! They're speaking to you, look!"

I look. Sitting in the five chairs were my five brothers having a drink among themselves. Their heads were bobbing like Chinese dolls'. And then suddenly everything dissolved. My tongue went to mush in my mouth.

"So they're—alive?" I whisper. "Alive, not all killed off? You mean, I'm *not* guilty? . . ."

"What difference does it make?" she answers. "Guilty, not guilty! Everybody is guilty of something!"

"And where're Mom and Dad? Are they here somewhere among us. . . ?"

Dora Aleksandrovna presses her finger to her lips. She doesn't utter a word, but the message comes through: my mother and father have gone far away from us, too far, and won't be coming back ever again. One—overwhelmed by the weight of great suffering. The other . . .

"Don't you worry about a thing!" she interrupts herself. Your brothers are here now and they don't plan on going anywhere. Take your time finishing your pie. Serve yourself whatever you please. Nobody will even notice!"

But I wasn't about to finish eating anything. I swigged down a couple of shots in order to bring myself into accord with reality, and took my place among the chairs. Everything cleared and crystallized before my eyes. Five brothers, exact replicas of Nikolai, Pavel, Vasily, Yakov, and Vladimir, were presiding over a table-top discussion about me, close enough to touch. Their words reached me through the thick partition, though with a considerable delay and with some difficulty, at times loud and at others completely inaudible. Dora, by my side, like a bride and groom, whispered to me and prompted me from time to time. My brother Nikolai opens his mouth: "All because of me. He drowned on a drinking binge. Threw himself overboard into the water after his poodle. We never did find him. I dove down again and again. . . ."

"You're wrong, Nikolai," Pavel objects thoughtfully. "Our little brother rotted away in Kolyma. And the poor thing was still hoping his dog would be waiting for him. . . ."

"You guys just sit here and don't know the first thing about it!" cuts in Yakov. "I had his number. I'm telling you, he had an inferiority complex that ended in a premature heart attack, even. Runs in the family. That Little Jinx never made it to adulthood."

"And our mother. . . ."

"His father's the one! His father!" bellowed Vladimir so loud that the dishes clattered. "If it weren't for that father of his, he wouldn't have fallen underneath the bus like your common everyday gawk! . . ."

I sat transfixed. From here on in they began moving their lips like fish under water and I couldn't make out a darn word. I turned to Dora to have her turn up the volume in our guests' speakers. But she says: "So you think they've come to attend the wedding? Dream on! They've come to attend your wake. And don't look so surprised! Here, allow me! . . ."

And she brushes some crumbs off my chair with her napkin. I notice that the chair is already empty. . . .

"You died. You died way back when. And so you're not here, get it? Before you were born. . . ."

I was at a complete loss. Of their speeches only fleeting fragments reached my ears. I do not, therefore, pretend to reproduce them in their entirety. We were placed, if you will, on the threshold of two opposing worlds. Dora and I were on one side of the chasm. My five brothers were on the other.

Ol' Volodya continued: "I could strangle his old man with my bare hands without batting an eye. He. . . ."

"What's *he* got to do with it? rebutted Yakov in his defense. "I know that Mama. . . ."

"A lot to do with it! He was a decadent. A sissy. In our times a writer must . . ." (Vasily).

"He rotted away on Kolyma! On Kolyma, I'm telling you!" (Pavel).

"No, no, no!" (Nikolai). "As a husband he could no longer satisfy her needs!"

"He could no longer satisfy the needs of his country!" (Vladimir).

"Of history! Of the age! . . . He was a total jinx, too!" (Not clear who, in the free-for-all).

How they roared with laughter! . . .

Suddenly everything grew dim, paling before my eyes, and rose aloft. That's what you get for a short while after drinking when you're out of practice. Walls, wineglasses, the brothers in their chairs, inexorably rose while they continued to sit and speak in judgment over my father and me—in the form of a tapestry with woven guests, musicians, and dancers. But you yourself slowly creep down underground, on the return train; yet all the same you are still of this world, in your seat. I'll try to describe it.

Getting off the bus, I strolled as usual along Khlebny Street to Apartment Bldg. No. 9, from which I was once removed fifty years ago and where, according to a former housing permit, there still lived a dog and a boy barely born to a widow whom I had recently divorced. This was the old return to the homestead. The final attempt to square things up. . . . It was late autumn. A wet snow fell like rain, melting before reaching the parvis. I guess you'd call it sleet. The flecks of snow evidently did not have time to feather out into transparent, star-shaped snowflakes. The white medley swirled listlessly in the air and perished in vain. It seemed as if the snow were not falling, but instead whirling upward into the evening sky, rising like a theater curtain silhouetted against the dark houses, which were in the meantime ever sinking into the ground. The roadway glistened like oil overflowing into a black sea from the gates of the Arbat to the gates of the Nikitsky, the even landslide of buildings sinking beneath my feet in the asphalt through the muslin curtain and turning into luminescent mud.

You've had the opportunity to observe a similar aberration somewhere in America, I suppose. An oak bartop and a bartender, white cups of coffee as black as a Negro; on a tray, attractive aperitifs suspended below a little faucet that looks like a parrot in a cage that is making for itself an interesting spectacle of the guests—they go soaring up to the ceiling. But we nocturnal birds come down periodically. The lower half of consciousness glides upward like an elevator, while the other half, like an adjacent elevator, comes sailing down. As soon as the bacchante makes her appearance onstage with a didactic and promptly assigned check mark in parentheses (the kind pedantic schoolteachers make in pupils' exercise-books), she keeps you in her sights, on the bull's-eye, with the acute triangle of her hips, without letting you stray upward or drop down. But you remain seated. . . .

"Writer? A bathroom-wall graffiti-artist!" came from the table.

To hell with mud-slinging. It was more important to me not to lose sight of my brothers, presiding judicially somewhere up on the ceiling while they were alive, theoretically, getting to the bottom of the murder. Now about that cabaret in America and that snowfall on Khlebny Street with my dumbfounded father barely coming through at the end of the simile, just imagine for the sake of clarity an escalator in Moscow's deep-sea metro. Today, upon my arrival, I had availed myself of such modern conveniences, and, as I recall, not without the timidity of an old-timer who had lost touch with Moscow, so I hazarded a step onto the uneven, corrugated walkway and was borne downward. . . .

The guests were being taxied by conveyor from the world beyond to meet the bloodless party of exhibits while we were plunging down the shaft, finding ourselves powerless to distance ourselves from or merge with the parallel flow, unconsciously scanning the hierarchy of wide-browed statues being erected from the bowels of the earth with their tensely propped profiles thrust forward as if they shunned intersecting with or accidentally running into our sinister stream, which was slowly and inexorably dispatching us underground. And who knows? The next time around we might have been able to swap places on the conveyor-belt; but for some reason that didn't dawn on anyone. Each kept to his own little stair, avoiding the opposite stream. Exchanging glances or greeting with a nod seemed out of the question.

The sole exception that aroused any interest was a certain (most likely independent) student, barely out of high school, very pretty, and painfully similar to that girl whom I lost somewhere in the past over a wisecrack. But we mustn't be too quick to put that Dora and this one in the same class. I had taken this girl for someone else. She wafted upward on the escalator, toward the sun and open air, which didn't stop her from bestowing, like an embrace, a hasty and passionate glance upon each passing passenger passively inching down the moving staircase, missing no one, quickly discarding the acquaintance of each conquest in favor of another, assured of her ascent from out of the scene of jealousy, gossip, and slander; inaccessible, exultant, securely soaring toward the heavens with a face sifted by the rivers of the dead, who already know that they would not meet her ever again. And were any of us, falling for the seduction, to chase back up the escalator after his ephemeral love, he would not be able to break his way through the dam of people in time to catch up with her anyway. And even if he did get through, the traitress would refuse to recognize him. Giving me the once-over, she wrote me off altogether, like a blank space, with a brusque, critical flip of the chin. And suddenly she nodded, smiled, invitingly jingled the bracelets on her delicate wrists at someone apparently just in back of me, some more deserving admirer. "Just who is this lucky guy?" I thought, and instinctively shot a sideward glance behind me. No one was in back of me on the escalator. Leaning forward and peering down from up on top, she motioned with a nod, laughed, and waved her handbag at my invisible companion. And she even shouted something like, "Hurry and come up here. We'll meet at the entrance of the metro! . . ." But there was no reply. . . .

I came to my senses. Everything in the newlywed apartment was as it should be. The cabinet, the ceiling, the banquet table. Suddenly my brothers' voices dinned in my ears like when someone clicks on the radio. A certain amount of static. Were they still talking about me? About my father? My ears strained to hear. They were shouting: "What a shit! . . . Weakling! . . . The cause of all our troubles. Art, you see. Artist, from Latin 'arse.' . . . Bungler. . . . Atheist! . . . Rotted away. . . . Finished himself off. . . . A case of insanity. . . . In the asylum. . . . The dog! . . . Enemy of the People! . . . Waiting patiently. . . . He deserved to be drowned. . . . Judas! . . . Drowned. . . . Drowned? That's a bunch of . . . ! . . . Dump truck. . . . Heart attack. A regular old seizure, I swear it! . . .

"Listen up a minute!" Dora leaned toward me in an elegant new coat, with some sort of miniature purse held in her gloves. "Goodbye, Little Jinx! I'm leaving and won't be coming back. Going on business. Look after the cabinet, will you? Keep up with the latest news. And don't try to find me in the grocery—I don't work there. . . ."

I ignored her icy kiss on my forehead—the way one kisses the dead. I didn't want to miss a thing.

". . . him in jail. . . . So he died, plain died. . . . Just one big nuis——. Black sheep. . . . But, you know, there was something about him. So what if . . . For peace on the entire ear——. . . . Long live. . . . Until nex——. . . . How nic——. . . Well, she dumped him and——. . . That happ—— . . . Who would have. . . ? You don't supp . . . 'P' . . . Re . . . La . . . Ti . . . Do. . . ."

Dawn was breaking. No guests, no wife at the table. Dora had disappeared as irrevocably as she had appeared. Only the cabinet stood in the corner, up on its hind legs. An empty wineglass lolled on the table. A fish-prong. The window. The tablecloth. I was a bereft, jaded, stuttering old man. Evil to a point, and good to a point. No father, nor the mother I had apparently driven to the grave. No dog. Only five brothers, like five fingers blackened on my hand as I wrapped up my work on the ream of pages written throughout the night. . . .